"Addison Cain writes dark in the most delicious of ways. This book is twisted, engaging, and eerily captivating. Addison weaves a unique world that took my breath away and kept me turning the pages. Her kick ass heroine is one I won't forget. 5 star read."

~ Alta Hensley, USA Today Bestselling author

"Addison Cain is THE author to make readers fall in love with Sci-fi Romance. Her craft is masterful, the sex is smoldering, and the characters are so real I feel I could touch them. 5 Otherworldly Stars."

~ Anita Gray, Amazon Bestselling Author

"I've always been a fan of strong heroines, and Sigil isn't just strong - she's a total badass. Dangerous, lethal, and more powerful than you would even guess, this book takes you on a whirlwind of sex and violence that leaves you panting for just one more page of Addison Cain's incredible skill in dark romance!"

~ Jennifer Bene, USA Today Bestselling author

Sigil

Part One of the Irdesi Empire Series

By
Addison Cain

©2016 Addison Cain

All rights reserved.

No part of the book may be reproduced or transmitted in any form or by any means, electronic or mechanical, including photocopying, recording, or by any information storage and retrieval system, without permission in writing from the author. The only exception is by a reviewer, who may quote short excerpts in a review.

This is a work of fiction. Names, characters, businesses, places, events and incidents are either the products of the author's imagination or used in a fictitious manner. Any resemblance to actual persons, living or dead, or actual events is purely coincidental.

Cover art by Najla Qamber Designs

IBSN: 978-1-950711-17-8

*This book is intended for adults only and contains scenes featuring total power exchange which may make some readers uncomfortable.

Chapter 1

Arden observed a drip of perspiration fall between the nearest collared human's cleavage. The enslaved female offered a tray topped with a cool, extravagant beverage, she had offered a smile, and she had offered stillness so he might inspect her. One sip from the silver cup, and the tartness faintly reminded him of old-Earth lemons. The smell reminded him of something a bit more carnal. Looking pointedly over the cup's rim, he smiled at his hostess, the Tessan lounging on her couch, and the emissary sipped again. Wry expression confirmed their mutual understanding. The Mistress of Pax was aware there had been no scan of the goblet for poison. The offering of good faith made the inky eyes of the smirking ruler narrow in approval.

"He has quite offered you up, hasn't he?" Drinta teased, taking a sip of her own frosty cup.

A deep breath of humid air, a pleased, practiced smile, and the guest genuflected. "Quite."

A low extended hum vibrated from the Tessan, her green scaled skin expanding and contracting to maintain the rattle. "Sovereign thinks to persuade me with gifts… and a silver-tongued emissary."

Golden head bowed subtly, he replied, "I have yet to offer gifts."

"But you will." Her brow ridges, with their small shapely spikes, rose in a very human gesture.

Arden pulled another breath of air that was too moist, too warm to be comfortable, running a quick appraisal over the grand view his seat allowed.

Two words: backspace shithole.

From the sly curve of scaled lips, it was clear the Mistress of Pax agreed. Pressing back into the plush couch, facing the man seated across from her, the tip of her tail swished and all pretense ended. "There are things I want."

"Sovereign will provide them," the envoy of the human Irdesian Empire assured her. "In exchange for absolute access to your byway."

"I don't deal in"—Drinta cocked her head, quick-moving lids shuttering around the black of her eyes— "absolutes."

Crossing an ankle over his knee, Arden played his role to perfection. "This is where you tell me, Mistress Drinta, how you wish to be treated in this interaction. Do I grovel? Is aggression more interesting to you? Threats? Negotiation could be amusing... for us both."

Drinta sat tranquilly, mirroring a predator's stillness. "The Tessan Authority finds your empire's growth in power unsettling. Offering access to a warmongering species might complicate my comfort."

"Your sisters have labeled you as an intergalactic felon, pretty Drinta. Your former piracy gave you an intriguing reputation. But decimating and systematically destroying the Uresa Quadrant..." Arden smiled, a beautiful thing on a face created to attract. "Now, the Tessan Authority wants your head in a box."

"Perhaps I was a bit overzealous in my younger days." Green shoulders shrugged, scales catching a trace of distant flashing light.

"And now you keep court here," Arden agreed, fully aware of her blood-soaked history and the purposelessness of her previous violence. She had killed for the pleasure, simply because she could, taunting intergalactic governments to rise up and stop her. But it had turned out to be more trouble than it was worth. With age came wisdom. Stealing Pax Station from the previous overseers had been her last great conquest. She would never give it up—not like the planets she'd brought to their knees and let slip away once she became bored. Here she was a god, controlling one of the most valuable resources in the galaxy—the byway—and its access that could slice across space in a matter of minutes.

Tolls made her rich, but she did not reinvest the money into her dilapidated space station. Arden could see she liked her mire just as it was.

For Drinta, it had never been a question of wealth; it was a desire for power. Pax was her trading floor—import, export, slaves, intelligence, contraband—everything was allowed so long as one paid the proper monetary homage.

"How many planets does he have now?" The hiss in her voice, how it stretched the words, was musical.

"Many..."

She smiled back, sharp teeth on display. "And your ships?"

"Are legion."

"Legion." The word rolled off Drinta's tongue. "Pretty expression."

Standing from his overly cushioned seat, Arden moved toward the energy barrier separating the Mistress's plush balcony from the dingy venue. Club Swelter, the perfect example of the ancient human idea of sin, functioned as the nucleus of Pax. Far more than an entertainment spot, the hollowed out hive was infested: Dregs fondled the dancers as they made their trade. Smugglers, stocking up on whatever illicit item could be found, amused themselves as they negotiated. Unsavory mercenaries for hire drank, and fought, and pissed in the corners. Junkers came for the coin of hauling off garbage and dragging back the second-hand parts required to maintain the station's life-support. The room was full of shouting voices who bartered and barked for what they were owed. But the most powerful in the station's den of iniquity were the slavers. They were always there; they were always abundant, delivering or purchasing new stock and raking in the profits.

Pax slaves, though illegal in many cultures, were coveted—considered to be broken perfectly. *The best.*

How fantastic the livestock was, considering the venue.

Drinta neglected the upkeep of the station; decks clung by a tether. On a regular basis, pieces of Pax fell off, floating away to orbit amidst a disturbing asteroid belt of garbage. Everything was dim and dank… yet the slaves were lovely. Every species, every gender, anything one might want in the form of living pleasure made available for the right price—always tempting, always on display.

Throughout Swelter, exotic creatures danced, writhing on their platforms, some available for patrons to touch and handle as they pleased, shadowed just enough to make fucking appear somewhat mysterious. *Enticing.*

Drinta's well-guarded balcony sat where she could easily enjoy the show—where her subjects could see her and never forget who was in charge. From the vantage, Arden took in the levels, surveying the debauchery. But it was not the nearest pleasure slaves, posing once they saw a guest of the Mistress look their way, who caught his attention. Golden eyes were drawn to one twisting her body in a distant swath of hanging red silk.

Painted limbs twirled, lean muscle manipulating her net in complicated figures.

The performer climbed dangerously high on that crimson drape, the slave suspended over her audience where one slip up would culminate in a messy fall to her death. Yet, she projected serenity, power, the daring acrobat spinning so fast the world from her eyes must have been only a blur.

And down she went, a river of flesh rippling over blood red silk, spinning, falling, torsion mangling her showcase.

It was beautiful, her figures promising fulfillment or ruination in that frantic descent. A breath from the floor she froze, toes pointed, limbs free, holding on to the fabric with nothing but one coiled leg.

Drinta eased beside the high-ranking human, eager to see what might pique the interest of the Imperial emissary. She too found the swath of red silk and the frozen spider tangled in it.

Ahh, yes... a human female. How ordinary.

Each passing flash of light and the observers took what they needed from the scene: the sheen of sweat when the performer shifted, slipping out of her drape to display nudity save a few scraps of black and her collar. Tranquility radiated from her, the slave smoothing plum colored hair from her face.

Without warning, the slave stopped preening and leapt from her platform to race through the leering crowd. Her target, a mountain of muscular Axirlan, stood stolid awaiting her approach, arms crossed over his bare chest.

Like others of his species, the huge male did not emote. He did not return her exuberance or expression. Humanoid, skin silvery white, larger than all around him, he exuded innate strength—his peoples' defining feature, something they broadcasted with little more than a ripple of movement.

The slave seemed undisturbed by the Axirlan's mass, his cold expression, or the fact he could break her in half with little more than a flick of his wrist. She looked only to adore, falling to her knees at his feet, eager, glowing, and ready to please.

"How sweet. The female is offering affection to her keeper." A small, amused curl came to sculpted angular lips, Drinta's eyes shining at the display. "Just watch and see how well our slaves are trained."

Without prompting, the human's nimble fingers undid the fastenings of the male's lower covering, pulling out a studded member already thickening and growing hard in her hands.

Decorated with a series of metal rods pierced horizontally, her keeper's cock caught the flashing lights until it disappeared into the human woman's mouth.

She smiled up into his eyes as she took his girth down her throat, serene as she carried out the sex act—as if only the two of them stood in the arena. All the while, her hands lovingly caressed hips, muscled buttocks, and even from a distance, Arden could see she swallowed to accommodate her keeper with every excited thrust the male pressed between her willing lips.

The way the giant stroked that mane of dark purple hair and watched her perform was so unlike an Axirlan. He was fond of his pet, to the extent an emotionless race could be.

Arden imagined he heard the groan as the beast threw his head back and climaxed, the burst of noise harmonizing with the blaring music. Watching the slave take that cock all the way into the recess of her mouth, the female gulping down silver ejaculate as it burst against the back of her throat, seeing her struggle to not spill a drop... excited the emissary.

When it was done, the Axirlan's massive, pierced organ popped from her lips. Her keeper swiped his thumb over them, brushing away the single drip that had escaped, silently praising her performance with his attention.

The woman sat back on her heels, panting and clearly contented, the shine of saliva smeared over her chin.

Arden studied her profile in the dark, the flawless symmetry of her features.

Though his face was impassive, he couldn't look away—not when she sought an embrace from her master and was gifted with more. The Axirlan cradled her to his chest and carried his pet to his table. After he sat, draped in pale human, her keeper conversed with others of his own kind.

And again, affection from the male: the brute toyed with her hair as she relaxed, was gentle with her.

Arden cut his gaze away, unsettled by what he sensed in the outlying corner. The woman was falling asleep in a very dangerous place, feeling safe in the arms of an oversized Axirlan she did not belong to.

No slave collar changed facts. If that was who he thought it was, she belonged to *him*.

After the endless chase—all the years—his Sovereign had never been able to corner her. And there she was, sucking off some alien for the entire crowd in that sleazy club on Pax to see, before napping like a spoiled cat.

Mistress Drinta turned her head just enough to let the light play across her fetching Tessan features. "If you like what you see, another with similar qualities could be arranged for you... as my gift."

The golden quality of Arden's expression matched the dulcet tenor of his question. "What of that one?"

A hand stretched out, flicking toward one of her guards so the underling might produce a data screen. Navigating livestock information, Drinta hummed. "I am afraid she is listed as private. I can't fault her keeper for that—not when she seems so very skilled and attentive."

Fingers snapped and Drinta commanded her guard, "Bring my guest a human pleasure slave. A pretty one with dark hair."

A beauty appeared so quickly it was apparent several were kept nearby, available should Drinta offer.

The Tessan's black lateral pupils darted back to the human delegate *sent by Sovereign himself* as she ordered the slave to, "Suck his cock."

There was no hesitation in the submissive young woman to fall to her knees and perform.

Arden's hand rested on the back of the girl's head, setting a pace as he envisioned the distant sleeping female, imagining another's lips and tongue working him well. He came quickly, sighing when he released into a stranger's mouth.

"Now that we've taken the edge off, let us continue negotiation." Drinta's voice was once again laced with her brand of enticement, the most dangerous criminal in the quadrant smiling broadly. "Your Sovereign and the empire he rules, what can they do for me?"

Drinta's choice of words was not lost on the emissary. What could Sovereign do for *her*? No, it was quite the other way around. Yet the man smiled richly, expressing his purpose on Pax. "The Irdesian Empire can offer you anything you desire." Leering, turning to face the showy female with her flicking tail, Arden neared. "Is there something you would like to have conquered? Old enemies you wish to see tormented?"

Her gaze drew deadly. "Yes. And he will deliver what I wish, or access to the byway will never be granted to his fleet for whatever little war you are waging now."

"I was ordered your wish is my command." And though his golden eyes glowed, his thoughts were gravely amused that the criminal queen actually believed she might deny his empire anything.

"I demand the entirety of the Ran 7 colony to be exterminated. Not converted, not enslaved; slaughtered."

"Consider it done."

She looked at him, a pleased mischievous dragon as she cooed, "There's more."

When dealing with that quality of lifeform, there was always more. Arden, Herald of the Irdesian Empire, smiled beautifully, promising the treacherous Mistress of Pax her heart's every desire.

Her heart was quite black.

Chapter 2

Stretching, purring with each pop of her spine, Quinn wriggled beneath the reclining giant's arm. Enjoying the familiar weight of the bulging appendage and the way the mattress dipped from Que's weight, she rolled and found he was awake, watching—expressionless.

Silver eyes set in a face white as snow, his features strongly angled and broad. "When you wake you always wish for me to fuck you."

Quinn's fingers slipped forward to trace from the hollow of his throat, between the mass of pectorals, and down the definition of a torso three times the size of hers. "You were gone for seventeen cycles."

"Do you desire to be fucked now?" The Axirlan queried again, ignoring her words as they had no real meaning, no point beyond stating facts.

She didn't answer, continuing to touch, contemplating a body almost as strong as hers.

"Speak, slave girl."

His taunt drew a wicked laugh from the human.

It had taken years to teach an Axirlan the nuances of sarcasm and humor. Though he may not understand the way another species' minds emoted, Que did make an effort to play to her nature.

Hand dipping lower, Quinn lifted the weight of his pierced erection. "I believe it might be quite the other way around."

Before she might blink, he pounced, Axirlan mass grinding caught prey against the bowing mattress. The deep, almost robotic base of his voice rumbled, vibrating through her skin as he said, "I think what you desire is a fight."

The dyed lavender of her eyes went languid. "I love when you fight me."

Burrowing his face in her neck, the broad flat of Que's tongue tasted the soft skin of his momentarily tame paramour. "You are a monster."

"I know," she sighed to the ceiling, enjoying the way his teeth found her throat, how he scraped her flesh just enough to sting.

It was her moan that enticed him to claw the softer places of her body, to dig nails in and break skin. Pain subdued her for an instant—long enough for Que to force the woman's legs apart.

Without preamble, he jammed the beauty of his cock balls deep before the slippery human might try to evade. Rooted, stretching her mercilessly, he left her neck to gnaw a nipple raw.

Crushed under the onslaught, Quinn grinned.

It was more than the rough handling and smell of blood. It was who was hurting her and why.

With strength that would have broken another, the Axirlan growled at the slick milking pull of her cunt greedily devouring his cock despite his aggression. Lost in the craze that made fucking an Axirlan so dangerous for one so small, he roared. Taking her by the neck, muscled arms bunched, the alien reared to watch every last sensation play over her face.

Bliss.

He could see it ripple under her skin, little shockwaves each time one of his piercings breached the slippery flesh of her pussy.

"You will wear my semen tonight when you dance." It was his right to demand such a thing, and he did so brutishly.

Dyed eyes rolled back into her skull.

He shifted with speed unique to his kind and placed a finger on the metal bar decorating the hood of her clitoris. His mark. One she had accepted years ago. "And I desire to penetrate you where all can see, your legs spread open over my lap, your piercing on display so Swelter might recognize what's mine."

She was so close, the whisperings of oblivion crackling like lightning in her bones.

The instant a building climax stole her breath, the female grew vicious.

Grinding joints, she overpowered the large male, manipulating Que's mass under her violence in a twist of limbs. The savagery in her expression, the abject threat as she began to sink down upon his aching member would have warned any other male to be still and obedient.

That was not Que's way. That is not what they were.

Muscles shaking in an attempt to indulge his human, he brutally bucked against her hold in search of his own release.

As pleasure peaked, she took his throat between her hands. Squeezing tendon and bone, damaging him, she drew out the dangerous male's first silvery spray of come.

Muscles shaking from the extreme effort required to draw her hips down, Que fought to hold her in place. She resisted, fluid seeped between them, scented the air, and Quinn cried out in those last hypnotic moments of completion.

When it was over, her fingers loosened about his abused throat, and she sagged onto the barrel of his chest. "For that fine performance I will submit any way you want, anywhere you wish."

Large fingers carded through a tangled length of plum hair. "That would please me, slave."

Snickering, she bit his nipple, sucking it hard before flicking the flesh with her tongue.

Under her gentler caress, the male grew pensive. "Do you long for more human interaction? Shall I tell you I love you?"

Placing her chin to his chest, Quinn smiled. "You are incapable of feeling such an emotion, my friend. There is no need to offer that expression."

A meaty hand gripped the back of her skull and pulled her upward until they were face to face. "If I could love you, I am certain I would."

Her heart grew warm. Yes, he had learned much. Pressing her forehead to his, she poured feeling into her words. "A beautiful thing to say."

"Then I have done well." A rich, unemotional rumble bade, "Now lie back. I am going to paint you. And then I wish to taste between your legs."

Obedient, Quinn slid off his torso and spread out on the smoothness of their sheets. "Yes, *master*."

⸺⸺

The markings of silver, the dried aftermath of Que's semen, swirled in patterns of his choosing all over her torso, breasts, and the front of her thighs. It was a very possessive gesture on his end, something that would be considered tawdry in places not quite as crude as Pax.

Her Axirlan was elsewhere on the station, attending to restocking his ship, which left Quinn to walk the corridors alone and untroubled.

There was power in the slave collar the overseers were too foolish to recognize—access to decrepit passageways, the ant farm of relegated districts—all available without question so long as a little strip of mechanics circled the throat and buzzed with each scan. Then there were the crawlspaces. Quinn took advantage of them regularly, acted the cockroach, creeping through filth anywhere she pleased.

The things she'd overheard in those passageways could topple governments.

Drinta had far too much faith in the all-consuming power of the collar to keep her thralls in line. But the horrors whispered amongst the enslaved population were true. One flick of a switch, one little prick, and the collar's bearer felt the burn of poison… until they felt nothing at all.

Tampering with the collar led to an incredibly painful and public execution. Examples were made regularly—more often than not, the slave innocent, used as a reminder to keep the rest groveling and licking the Tessan bitch-queen's boots.

Fear of the constant pinching reminder about one's neck, that's what truly controlled Pax slaves. For that reason, there had not been an uprising in almost four decades. Mistress Drinta's answer to the previous riots had been to simply flip the switch and kill every single slave on the station. Thousands had died, even children, their bodies carelessly dumped into space.

Echoes of the mass genocide still haunted the station. If one stood at the portholes and looked out over the circling debris, sharp eyes might spot bone, a corpse—fragments of what had once been a living creature. The visual reminder, the stories, were more than enough to keep the slave culture self-policing… as if *that* would prevent another holocaust.

Sneeze wrong and you were reported.

Moral of the story: trust no one, especially the slaves.

Drinta had them right where she wanted with hardly any effort exerted on her end.

Thousands bent the knee, even Quinn for show. But if someone pushed, annoyed, or just looked at her with a trace of doubt in their minds, Quinn had no problem jettisoning troublemakers out into space. Pax was *her* playground, and Quinn wore her collar with pride.

It was perfect, this life Que had designed for her. No one paid any attention to a pleasure slave, not on Pax where they were common. It was the traders who were constantly surveilled—the junkers, smugglers, anyone who came free—not the slaves. Because of the collar, Quinn had been able to marginally relax, settling peacefully into quasi-civilization for the first time in years.

Long haul space flight had lost its appeal ages ago. She far preferred society—or perhaps borderline anarchy would better describe Pax. The outer reaches of this volatile quadrant kept Quinn distant from the thing she fought every waking moment to avoid... away from temptation.

Her born addiction.

Quinn had demons.

Quinn had urges strong enough to sweep her into madness.

The constant physical activity of dancing at Swelter was a welcome distraction. The opportunity to rip apart a few spacer scum when she felt bloodthirsty helped ease the compulsion.

Pax was perfect, and she wanted to stay as long as she could.

Pax kept her separated from *them*.

The Irdesian Empire had no cause to pursue her beyond the Tessan Authority's furthest border zones—not when their goal was absolute human conversion. Not when free governments still resisted closer to their systems. They wanted her dead, she knew that. She was a threat to the emperor, to his Brothers.

They wanted her dead because she knew the greatest secret in the universe.

She knew what *they* really were.

She knew what they tasted like.

She knew how to break them apart, how to draw their blood, and how to disembowel each one. She knew exactly how to tear their world apart.

One glimpse of an Imperial and her mind shut off. The base, broken part of her took over. Hunt. Kill. Repeat. Over and over, mindless in the destruction. A slave to her compulsion. A slave of programming.

The problem was, she didn't know how to stop.

Que did.

Que kept her sane, met her baser needs. He had even given her a new name, one she found endearing, as it was so close to his own. Her possessive little—or she should say, lumbering and huge—Que.

The Axirlan male could snap a neck with one hand, almost as quickly as she could. He was a fine warrior and an even better comrade. The battles they had fought side by side, the savagery of what he was capable of, she had never found another to compare.

The male was also incredibly cunning.

The nature of their life on Pax had been his idea: master and slave. A game and a cover.

Que labored as a junker, selling scrap the station desperately needed to patch hulls. She bowed as the eager slave and danced to supplement her master's income.

In their years of peace residing on Pax, there had never once been a raised brow or question that could not be killed.

Pax was the perfect home for a psychopath and her savior.

It was also the perfect place to bury things no soul would miss.

Children.

Quinn had a great fondness for them. Those she favored the most, she took.

She stole them from their families and Keepers, and gave them something better.

Contorting her body to fit down the last, tight crawlspace, she came upon the hiding place of her dearest prize. Under scrap swiftly tossed aside, a cryotube waited, full of her latest foundling. While stroking the plastoglass, her eyes ran over the features of a little male Tessan with his yellow scales and elongated jaw sleeping inside.

Little Jerla.

What would it be like for him to wake up and be free, to feel sunlight filtered through an atmosphere warming his scales for the first time? Living with his own kind instead of ignored by an apathetic mother who found the gift of new life only another burden to contend with.

Quinn had wanted him at once, had secretly watched over him for years until he was old enough to set free.

Someday many years from now, she might find him happy and free, and tell the Tessan who she was.

Would he hate her for what she did? It didn't matter. Slavery was… undesirable for innocents. She knew that well enough. Furthermore, smuggling slaves off the station was so easy it was laughable.

A body in full stasis registered a lack of a heartbeat, the collar listing the slave as deceased. So long as life signs were off a few days, system tracking shut off. Collars were never recycled, therefore, they were never collected from a corpse. Bodies were simply left where they fell until someone dumped them out the garbage chute into space.

Unless a slave was prized by the owner, inquiries were hardly ever made. Useless children who were too young to serve, required maintenance the Keepers on Pax seldom desired to offer.

Every trip Que made off-station he would fill up on random scrap. On occasion, inside the garbage might be hidden a cryotube. It left full and returned empty.

Over and over, with the station none the wiser.

Daydreaming, smiling softly to herself, Quinn pet the glass and thought of her long dead mother. She had once done this for her. She was the first Quinn had stolen, the first sealed away from the world, and the first dragged off so she might die free.

Quinn had freed them both that day, standing victorious over those who'd made them slaves. And more importantly, she'd stood victorious over her own nature to do it.

Pressing her cheek to the plastoglass, Quinn lowered her lashes, remembering with joy her long-ago escape from the humans.

It was a lullaby, reliving the sounds of her handlers' screams. All her years of training used against them, the tactile gratification of ripping doctors in half, still fresh. Silencing their poking needles and endless torments forever. Then there were the other slaves, *Sovereign's sheep*, and how they had gaped at her parade... Some had even tried to get in her way.

She had let the sheep live, just to make the point that she could, then left the nightmare behind.

Chapter 3

"Sovereign, everything is proceeding as you commanded." Arden bowed to the communicator, his distant projection back in the capital a display of reverence to the greatest among them. "However, I suggest you find time to visit Pax immediately."

Sovereign's haunting voice veiled any surprise such an unusual request might have inspired. He was purely cold, direct. *"For what purpose?"*

"There is a female performing in Drinta's club. Though it was from a distance and I had only a brief glimpse of her, I have my suspicions. As I am under constant surveillance, I have made no effort to confirm them."

Through the speaker, the emperor's voice altered completely. Cautious, yet aggressive and hungry, he demanded, *"You believe Sigil is there?"*

"I have not seen her since the destruction of Condor. If it was her, she has altered her coloring. She was painted... and collared as the pleasure slave owned by an Axirlan Keeper. Given the circumstances, I may be incorrect, but my reaction to the female's presence was atypical."

Even with Sovereign galaxies away, Arden could feel the wheels in his leader's mind turning.

"Has it become public knowledge a contingent from our empire visits Pax?"

"No, Brother. Furthermore, I watched her fall asleep on the lap of her attentive Keeper. If it was Sigil, she had no idea a Herald was in the room. She was abnormally calm."

The com buzzed. *"Attentive?"*

Arden's cheek twitched. The topic of Sigil was a sore one, her continued escape something not to be mocked. "She greeted him with exuberance and a public act of fellatio. For an Axirlan, it was clear he was satisfied. He was also familiar in how he handled her."

There was a long, painful silence before the emperor spoke. *"My arrival is imminent."*

"I may be incorrect, Brother." Arlen admitted, still unsure, aware there would be complications either way.

"I would be very disappointed to find you were."

Nodding at the judgment, Arden asked, "And Drinta's demands?"

The Herald did not need to see his ruler to know the man had just cracked a dangerous smirk; it was all there in the music of his reply. *"Give her whatever she wants."*

"The list is mildly ridiculous, sir."

"I'm counting on it, Arden. Sovereign out."

"And what have you uncovered?" The edge in her sultry purr dangerous, Drinta made it clear she was unsatisfied.

Chiming music resonated from elongated, honed vocal cords, the pathetic creature before her half-starved yet tranquil. "Emissary Arden is a Herald."

An annoyed hiss and Drinta stalked closer to her captive. "I know he's a Herald, his rank was never in question! I do not pay you to waste words. I do not pay you to waste my time."

"You do not pay me at all." The grey Kilactarin male dipped his long neck, the picture of calm despite the killer before him.

A smile distorted her sneer, Drinta taking in the cramped enclosure hidden below the balcony where all meetings with the Mistress of Pax took place. "Each inhalation I allow, each morsel that extends your ponderous life, is payment."

"He is an ocean."

The Tessan wanted to roll her eyes at the metaphysical banter of a bland species only useful for their mental specialties and long memories. "He is a human. They are greedy and simple. They want things…" A talon, painted black, scratched at the soft skin under her favorite pet's fleshy throat in warning. "Be useful to me."

"The human's mind is… resistant to the type of reconnaissance you wish. The one known as Arden has no flicker beyond tediousness or resolve. The tediousness is ordinary. You bore him. The resolve is impressive. He does want something... badly."

"And this want"—the little spines ridging her brow angled upward, Drinta eager for the slim chance a human of Arden's influence could be corrupted—"is outside or inside the realm of his purpose here?"

A clicking sound, tusks rubbing in a thoughtful gesture, her captive asked, "What is his purpose?"

Dealing with such a philosophical race was trying at best, navigating their infuriating need to preach, a thousand times worse. If her slave circled back to existential, self-righteous Kilactarin babble, she would kill him for sport.

Drinta ran her tongue over the sharp edges of her teeth, blinking at the eyeless creature, the smooth oblong cranium that saw... in other ways. "If you answer my question with another question, I will rip the sensory node straight from your skull. You are *replaceable*."

"He finds your interactions interesting beyond the normal scope of his duty."

"You claimed I bore him." At last, something worthy. Drinta's pleasured murmur cooed, "Elaborate."

The male's lengthy neck undulated over slender shoulders, his skull angling upward as if drinking the air. "The human species is so fleeting. Time after time they have overbred into unsustainability, even to the point of destroying their home planet and fragmenting their kind through space. Why?"

Drinta's talon dug deeper into the Kilactarin flesh, warning there would be no long-winded history lessons, no philosophy. One solitary drop of yellow blood slipped down her finger, the Kilactarin hardly affected by the pain.

The male's voice chimed in a tone that made the answer seem obvious. "A primitive's desire."

Merciless eyes glittered, amused that the slave termed a far more successful galactic species primitive. "Sex."

"Reproduction," he corrected. "Offspring."

The tip of her claw retreated, Drinta licking the smear of yellow while she pondered the revelation.

Arden's duty on Pax. Offspring. What was the correlation?

Ignoring her prize pet as he retook his meditative posture on the floor, Drinta affirmed once again that Tessan gut instinct was far more valuable than a species who could only measure empathic observation and probabilities. The Kilactarin were as blind in foresight as they were in body.

A new fleet arrival had bumped the exit schedule of all departing vessels through the byway forward by a cycle.

Alteration to the timeframe made the pickup and exchange of cryotubes hazardous. It also meant Que had to leave his Quinn sooner than they had arranged, the Axirlan possessing no way to notify the female beyond a brief recorded message.

She was often alone on Pax, did well in solitude without a protector, but it was always a little dangerous to leave Quinn on her own.

Dangerous for others.

He'd observed her totally lose her composure only twice in the decades of their partnership, but it was enough to keep the Axirlan cautious.

In a temper, he had seen Quinn single handedly rip apart a freighter and everyone inside in a single psionic burst. And the human woman was very touchy about the handling of child slaves. When she discovered the Tessan boy's cryotube was still on Pax, she would not be happy. It could lead to complications.

Such reactions were the reason Que's people stood superior.

Emotions were dangerous.

It had taken the Axirlan *years* to tame her, to break her habit of simply taking whatever she wanted because she could. She had needed a purpose; he created one for her. And in turn, her existence gave him purpose. Since the universe had aligned them, their lives had been enriched. He was fortunate to find a companion who did not possess the minuscule lifespan of a typical frail human. They had already shared almost a century of Earth time together, though she had slept through several decades when it was necessary.

It was cyclical. Quinn's physiology would drain her of all energy, forcing her into a deep sleep that sometimes lasted years. On more than one occasion, Que had preemptively cajoled her into a cryotube when her behavior grew erratic.

Yet even in her hibernation there was something fulfilling in having her all to himself. Vulnerable in cryo, he knew she had faith in him to watch over her until she could be trusted to control herself. A new landscape always helped, a new cycle far from the humans she struggled to avoid.

Life on Pax was hard, it was uncomfortable. It was the perfect distraction for her. It also offered access to the byway in case she felt the need to flee. He'd lost her a few times in situations such as those. Of course he always found her. They were wired on the same wavelength. Sometimes she came willingly when he called. Other times it required—urging. Fortunately for him, the best way to pacify her was to fuck her.

Six different times he'd had to shoot her first and take her as she was bleeding. When she was weakened and mounted, the bloodlust would slowly fade until her mind grew soothed.

There was no other coitus he'd ever known like hers. Sometimes it almost seemed he could feel what she offered beyond the sexual urge and physical gratification. She loved the aggression displayed by his species in sex, never once questioned his methods, begged or commanded depending on her mood.

In her far more promiscuous days, he'd sat back and watched her experiment with a multitude of partners. It was always a beautiful show, but none made her sing no matter how rough they had been. They were all too weak; she was too strong. Others did not fulfill her in any capacity beyond transient physical pleasure.

Amongst his species, long-term human companions were unheard of. They were too frail. But they could bear children and were sometimes kept for that purpose—which made her posing as a slave believable. Yet the gods had never seen fit to grant him offspring with his human, no matter the offerings or prayers given.

Que had never voiced this concern to her, but once he had laid the warmth of his palm over her womb as he pumped his seed into her body, vocally entreating his gods for a child.

The look on her face...

Que did not understand emotion, but he knew the expression for human heartbreak. His warrior had felt vulnerable. He'd inexplicitly weakened her when his role was to make her stronger. In that tick of time, he'd thought he might comprehend the sensation of regret.

It had never happened again.

In the decades since, Que had ascertained certain topics about his companion were best understood by observation. She was sterile and she had not known until he'd put the realization of his long unfulfilled desire into her head. For a creature with so much power, to be powerless in that very basic way led her to do some strange things.

Her obsession with slave children, how she watched them, furtively saw to them as if he didn't notice was one such example. Quinn also went through cycles where she impulsively collected little trinkets, hanging things about to make her quarters appealing. Often times such behavior was a precursor to a loss of composure.

She would grow edgy, snappish, would confess to a craving to hunt far more than she already struggled with. Each time Que put her in cryostasis before she might have a provoked psionic episode or mechanically go on the warpath. A few years monitoring her brain waves, and once her system regulated, he would wake her and she would smile.

Que preferred her smiles to the frowns. The female's expressions were intriguing, but the smile was worth the effort to draw out. The sound of her laughter was also enjoyable, the shriek of her yelling far less pleasant. Fortunately, it was something she seldom directed at him.

Once this next twenty-five cycle interval of their separation was complete, Que decided he would bring her a gift to earn a smile—perhaps a pet or the colorful reproductive portions of a plant.

Chapter 4

A large party of Sudenovan mercenaries had gathered near her platform to drink heavily and boast of their prowess.

Hanging upside down from the stage's fabric, Quinn trained her attention on the bristling males and tried not to sneer. With battle-marred armor and the stink of various species' sexual fluids mixing with unwashed Sudenovan, they were disgusting. Already arguing amongst themselves, all it would take was for one to reach for their weapon and all hell would break loose.

But it was more than just the riled males—Swelter was teeming with mercs, rival gangs, criminals, the room simmering with an alarming combination of villains.

When a fight broke out—and it would—the numbers would be thinned, but as packed as Pax was, riots might follow that could harm her delicate home. Glancing to Drinta's balcony, Quinn found the Tessan watching, amused, as if taking in a performance piece. The bitch-queen should have named the dump 'The Coliseum' considering how much she enjoyed lording it over the contenders of her pit. Then again, that was a human word, and Drinta was a reptilian, cold-blooded creature, hatched far from the Imperial colonized system where old Earth rotted as it swung around a dying star.

Spinning down the fabric, toes pointed and body arched, Quinn landed on the black lacquered slice of shadow. Eyeballing the crowd, she could not help but be troubled. There were too many newly blooded mercenaries gathered below—the balance purposefully off—and Drinta, she looked positively gleeful standing over a powder keg that could rip Pax apart.

An army had been mustered, patched together from anyone with ties, with debts, or who sought to gain from the Mistress of Pax. The bitch-queen had called in favors.

Something was going on.

Quinn had heard no rumors, sensed nothing in those around her except the usual: greed and desire to get their dicks wet... or whatever sex organ they had. There was a lack of anticipation which accompanied impending war. The patrons seemed bored, others just hungry, some of the more important guests she found oddly irritated to be there.

No, the congregation was not in preparation of battle. But the Tessan mistress was taking a calculated risk allowing so many conflicting species, guilds, and criminals to collect... as if she were demonstrating just what kind of nightmare she could call on.

What prompted such a display of power?

Hatred for politics aside, the answer mattered. Quinn found Drinta necessary. The Tessan was skilled in keeping the violence in balance and keeping Pax running. Should the bitch-queen lose the station, any other who took her place might not be so easy to live with.

A new ruler might ruin Quinn's serenity, force her to leave.

So, what figure would inspire Drinta to draw such an unruly crowd to such an unstable place?

If the answer was the one itching at the back of Quinn's thoughts, she would have to flee, and Que was not there to follow her.

Running without him... sometimes she'd lose her way.

Once it had taken him six years to find her. The things she'd done without his influence had not been her proudest moments. She'd slaughtered an entire penal colony some bounty hunter had been foolish enough to dump her in. Long gone by the time the asshole who'd offered an outrageous reward might fetch her, the only things she'd left behind were wreckage and the dead. Her regret was not in killing so many horrible men and women.

It was that once she'd started, she couldn't stop.

She'd left the rot and gone after gangs, bandits, unsavory governments... rampaged until Que found her. Thousands had died simply because she was *in a mood*.

Loss of control made her just like them—one of the sheep.

Pinching the bridge of her nose, Quinn slunk back into the dark, out of sight of the customers, and began to worry. It had been only three cycles since Que had gone and he would not be back to share his wisdom for twenty-two more. Her Axirlan always had a sense about these things. Should her anxiety be unfounded, he would reassure her. If she was correct, in perfect calm he would take her away, and together they would start all over again somewhere new.

But she enjoyed Pax. Quinn would rather not leave.

"Are you feeling all right?"

Glancing at an unfamiliar male pleasure slave, Quinn gave a dry, "No."

The unknown furrowed his brow. "Don't let them see you hiding. You'll get the lash."

There was something so ironic in the ancient way slaves were punished on Pax. She might actually like the lash. "Who are you?"

"Sasha."

Annoyed, Quinn reached for the vial of water in his hands and sucked it down as if it had been hers to take. "Sasha is not your name. Sasha is the name of the slave I usually perform with."

The near naked man shrugged. "I was told it would be easier for the patrons to recognize my place if I took the name of the one who was sold."

"Of course you were." Quinn had liked original Sasha—he was mute. "What *was* your name?"

"Sasha."

"Well, *Sasha*." She drank the rest of his water. "Welcome to Swelter."

"I've worked in worse places..."

Doubtful.

A pretty smile came across the man's dimpled cheeks. "Come on. My keeper is in the crowd."

She took his offered hand and let him tug her to standing. For a human mind, especially one of a slave, the male's thinking seemed a bit too sharp.

Sharp humans didn't dance like sluts on stages for kicks. Sharp humans didn't wear a slave collar—they either died trying to be free or were never caught in the first place.

He didn't smell of the Empire, nor did she sense he knew who she was. But he made her nervous. The whole fucking room made her nervous.

Quinn knew well enough that a nervous Quinn was a weak Quinn.

Lips curved into a friendly smirk, Quinn asked, "Were you collared as a child, new Sasha?"

The answer of, "Yes," was paired with a dazzling grin displaying white teeth against ebony skin.

He was lying. Whoever new Sasha was, he was no more of a slave than she.

Sucking her bottom lip between her teeth, Quinn did not release his hand. Stronger than she appeared, she ever so slowly pulled the male near, sniffed him, tempted to stretch out her tongue for a taste.

The moment grew awkward, uncomfortable, until the man's cheerfulness diminished.

She leaned closer. "You have the grip of a true aerialist. I'm eager to see what you can do."

The dimples came back, his eyes lost their fear, and he boasted as men do. "Just try to keep up with me."

Snickering, tugging him towards the partition to retake the stage, they appeared hand in hand, beautiful and grand. Twenty minutes later, the new Sasha was a heap on the ground… neck broken from a terrible fall.

Quinn played the shocked slave, sliding down her fabric showcase to be quickly contained by an overseer.

There was little commotion as the fresh corpse was dragged away by an ankle. No one in the crowd seemed to care; no keeper complained.

He may have had nothing to do with her, he may have been security or a spy for Drinta's crowd, but new Sasha was an unsettling factor. In Quinn's experience, unsettling factors had to be removed *immediately*.

As soon as the stage was cleared, she was shoved back up by a rough Tessan overseer who felt free to fondle her in the process. Quinn didn't mind it one bit.

She could cut the overseer's throat while he was sleeping if she wanted to.

She didn't.

For the following hours, she performed alone, watching the crowd watch her. It was almost possible to forget the nagging sensation in her belly.

Or it was until the rumble of ships through the byway stopped jolting the station.

The intoxicated masses did not seem to notice the loss of vibration over the blaring music. Either that, or they didn't care the very heartbeat of Pax had stopped.

No one in. No one out.

Closing her eyes, Quinn pulled in a breath, reminding herself to remain calm. After all, the probability that it had anything to do with her was incredibly slim. Pax was in the middle of inhospitable space, far from the sheep. Swelter was not a hub; it was an end destination for disreputables like her. The distant Irdesian Empire, there was nothing on Pax for them—not even nearby human planets to convert to their power.

Her paranoia was misplaced, that's what Que would tell her.

So why shut down the byway? Why pack the crumbling station with creatures itching for a fight?

As if the universe offered an answer to her question, the long simmering brawl began.

Shots were fired, tables thrown. Slinking down, Quinn kept a keen eye on the perpetrators, on drunks who engaged, on factions, in search of a pattern, a hint. The waving surge of reptilian Tessan, the emotionless Axirlan killers, the squat powerhouses of Sudenovan warriors with their tusks and war calls—not to mention the human traffickers—began to expend built up aggression, seemingly enjoying the fight as much as they had enjoyed the show. Nothing more.

There was no organized coup.

Half veiled by the long red spider silk, Quinn's eyes went to the mistress's balcony. Drinta was frowning, her tail swishing at her back. The Tessan was intensely aggravated when she should have been pleased by the carnage and show it supplied.

It took only one breath for Quinn to recognize her mistake.

Everything, all of it, had been a clever distraction.

The aggression of the horde, the suspicious new dancer, all fed to her by a brilliant tactician in order to keep Quinn looking in all the wrong places when she was uneasy—to keep her questioning and in Swelter when she should have been stealing the nearest ship and jetting off into hyperspace.

Her life here was over.

The masterful rumble of a smooth tenor came from behind. "Either you can go to him, or he will come for you."

Turning, the muscles in her neck strained by the effort it took to move slowly, violet eyes found a face of great beauty standing in the shadows—a Herald so close, all she had to do was take five steps and his neck would be in her grip.

She could rip it right off his shoulders…

Words were spoken softly, Quinn fighting to maintain a temperate composure. "Is it that you want to die?"

The Herald stood solemn, golden, as he spoke again. "He is waiting."

The image of the man in question crept to the forefront of Quinn's thoughts, every detail flawlessly remembered. Only once had she seen him in person, down a long corridor deep within the compound where they had been created, tested, educated, and used: Condor.

During the long ago glimpse, her body had still been that of a child's, the male full grown, but the second her prey was in her sights, her undeveloped form had seen nothing but him.

She'd had his attention as well, every part of the man focused on the little girl designed and trained to kill him. All those decades ago, he'd had the nerve to look upon his one-day assassin as if fascinated.

He'd even looked at her tenderly.

Quinn's handlers had reacted in a panic at the unintended meeting, the small hallway between her and the man thick with tension, drawn weapons, and loud voices.

They'd anticipated violence. As a girl, she'd loved to circumvent their expectations in ways which kept them questioning. So, she'd turned her head and walked away, increasing the confusion—because unlike that asshole, she wasn't a sheep who did as she was told.

She'd made herself greater than her programing.

"Tell your Sovereign I told him to fuck off." In an odd way, the warning was well meant, even passed forward in a tone of voice that affected self-control.

It was ten times harder to turn away from temptation in that moment than it had been over a century ago, yet somehow she managed to tear her eyes from the Herald instead of ripping him apart as she'd been trained to do.

The hitch in her step, the near stumble, betrayed her struggle for composure. Under her own power, fighting the compulsion to instantly hunt and slaughter, Quinn slipped through the brawl and out of the chaos in Swelter.

Chapter 5

The hallways were as mad as the club. Fist fights, ozone stink lingering from provoked laser blasts, and pained death-wails bounced off the cylindrical walls.

All of it ignored by the unblinking woman.

Dodging sweaty bodies forced Quinn to focus, but each bump of her shoulder, each leer, roused the monster. Those who tried to take advantage of a solitary pleasure slave found no mercy.

Her kills were clean, mechanical, unfulfilling in their quickness. They had to be. Indulging in savagery would only feed her desire to rampage.

Remove the obstacle. Control herself. Flee.

Single mindedness, focus when weak, that's what Que had taught her. That is what she struggled to achieve.

But it was almost impossible.

Quinn was exceedingly careful, breathing in a steady rhythm, ignoring what clawed its way around her insides—the compulsion—the itch to seek out Sovereign and break every bone in his body.

It was the wrath that blinded her to how truly exposed she was.

As she progressed through Pax, Quinn began to scream her frustration at the offense, uncaring who heard her rage that Sovereign still pursued even after so many decades. That he dared, after the amount of carnage she'd left for him to find. A warning when the bastard had pressed too hard or she had carelessly come too close.

Measuring inhalations, calculating the options available, she moved in a lizard's path through the corridors. With the byway offline, possible escapes were limited. In a stolen ship, under stasis, she could drift through the stars. But it would take years to reach any destination the Empire wouldn't think to search, she would lose Que, and chances of interception were incredibly high should Sovereign have ships at Pax under his power.

Then there was her cryotube full of the little Tessan boy. She could sleep there, costing the stolen child his future and his life. As the pod was still in sensor range, the second the Tessan's heart began to beat, the collar would activate and kill him.

She could not do that. Sovereign would find her in a floor by floor search anyway.

With the ravenous burn growing in her veins, one thing seemed inevitable—the thing she was foaming at the mouth for. It was time to face her quarry, where she would kill him, and then snuff out every life on Pax once the bloodlust took over.

Blinking, something wet fell down her cheek. Quinn wiped it away, pressing her back to the slimy corridor wall in anguish.

Another mindless rampage... she couldn't allow it.

Her life on Pax was over, her decade of near peace and all future years at an end. There was only one worthy option. She would offer herself up before she lost her crumbling strength of mind. Sovereign would finally kill her, tens of thousands of lives would continue, and she would not become a mindless slave to impulse.

A roll in her gut and Quinn found she could practically taste his trail, and followed the echo of him all the way to her rooms. Outside her dwelling, she meticulously cracked her neck, trying to remember all Que had taught her.

Freedom required constant control. Constant control required diligence. Diligence was enforced by calm.

But Quinn was not calm.

She felt cornered. Angry. Mostly she felt the need to open the door and launch her body at the tyrant. After all, shouldn't he, too, have to face consequences and suffer? Quinn had given him a hundred years of life. Clearly they'd been taken for granted if Sovereign was foolish enough to trap himself on a derelict space station with her.

The male was practically begging for it.

Biting down on her lower lip, Quinn pressed the access panel. The door slipped open, and she swallowed the accumulating taste of blood.

It was dim the instant the portal locked behind her, but he was there. She could smell the scent of running water, of cooling things. She could smell him.

From the shadows came approval. "I am pleased you have not tried to run."

She'd never heard his voice in person, only sound bites from training days of the male barking orders or outlining reports... the noises he'd made when fucking supplied females. There was a pleasing quality to it which belied the ferocity of the monster—a voice designed to charm and coerce, like a dancing serpent drawing one nearer so he might fill you with venom.

Turning up the lights, she found him standing proudly, posing for her at attention, unsmiling but radiating satisfaction.

Like the others of his kind, he was unfailingly beautiful—part of the lure that made them so dangerous in so many ways. Black hair had grown long since she'd last seen him, tucked behind his ears and waving to his jaw. He also bore the shadow of stubble, more casual than the commanding clean-cut necessity of a dead nation's perfect crafted soldier.

Her eyes lingered over the contours of his face, explored the column of his structural weak point—his exposed throat.

A wiser man would have worn armor, not the stark black uniform of the Empire.

Sovereign took a step.

"It would be in your best interest to keep your distance. Otherwise you may find how very difficult it is for me to control my urge to butcher you."

"Sigil." He sang her name, eyes a perfect storm while taking her in as if he'd been starved for the sight.

She hated that designation.

Showing teeth, she hissed, "My name is Quinn."

"Your name"—imperiously, he stepped nearer—"is Sigil. The title far more than the project for which you were fashioned. It's what you are: inscribed genetics. A creation of perfection."

"Perfection?" She gave an unimpressed snort. "That is exactly how I should appear to you." Eyeing him as if he were a fool, Quinn sneered. "The shade of my skin in line with your preference. Each curve of my body designed to mimic the females you took the most pleasure in. Everything from the size of my breasts to the natural color of my hair and eyes, all created to draw *you* in—making it much easier for me to assassinate you, had Commander Demetri felt the need to unleash me on a programmed slave soldier who'd grown too autonomous." Her chin lowered to her chest. "So why do you tempt me to do what long-dead men and a depraved, horrible society desired?"

"I can see the sparks between your fingers—the automatic buildup of psionic energy." He took another step closer and asked, "Are you struggling for control?"

"Yes." Her fists tightened until the bones in her fingers popped. Psionics drained away, and Quinn made the offer of her life. "You would do well to end this now before I slip and punish you for hounding me."

"And how would you punish me?" The weight of his gaze, the curiosity he did not hide, seemed backward—as if he the wolf and she the sheep.

Shoulder blades met the corroded wall at her back, Quinn purring, "You have pretty eyes. Maybe I will collect one."

The man nodded, his presence commanding far too much space. "Then come nearer, Sigil."

Something about his tone was... wrong.

Her eyes narrowed.

Advancing until he stood before her, tall, broad, Sovereign looked down at her upturned face as if it were his due.

Practically humming with the need to tear out his entrails, Quinn's hand moved on its own. She reached for his throat.

Sovereign allowed it, even lifting his chin to give her better access.

Graceful fingers wrapped around warm skin. All she had to do was squeeze and she could crush his windpipe. Or better yet, claw right into the lovely pulsing artery under her thumb and tear out a handful of flesh.

Her nail dug in, a sensation of pleasure flooding her body.

Indifferent to the threat, Sovereign fingered her slave collar. "I absolutely abhor seeing this around your neck, precious Sigil. Whatever game you have been playing that requires a collar, it's over now."

Insulted at his use of an endearment, the hand wrapped so beautifully around Sovereign's throat tightened.

Eager to watch him choke, anticipating the beauty of the man forced to kneel before her, Quinn envisioned plucking out one of his unimaginable eyes and crushing it to jelly—or maybe eating it, swallowing down a piece of him while he watched.

The fantasy blossomed, made her smile, and she slipped further into manic bloodlust.

Sovereign slowly, deliberately wrapped his fingers around her wrist.

Applying strength he should not possess, he forced her shaking grip from his throat.

Shocked out of her burgeoning fantasy, Quinn gasped.

Struggling unsuccessfully to regain the limb he'd claimed, her effort earned only a tick from his jaw.

Sovereign maintained his hold.

She'd been created to be better than him—superior. But despite straining muscles, she could not move her arm.

Pressing his greater mass forward, the man flattened her against the wall.

"Program Cataclysm, the classified creation of genetically perfected humanoid soldiers, assassins, infiltrators, decimators. I was created to lead that army." The bastard lectured, unsmiling features intense as he kept her restrained. "In the decades before your birth, under the orders of Commander Demetri, your Brothers conquered colonies, neighboring planets, whole systems—any civilization that stood in the path of the Alliance—so effectively, the foolish humans began to realize just how superior their creations really were.

"Leadership began to question why every prevailing galactic society had made genetic genesis taboo. Furthermore, had other species learned humans had experimented on their own kind, mutilated their coding to steal their uniqueness to create superior *human* slaves, it would have started an intergalactic war. The humans would have been eradicated, as they were still weak, constantly feuding amongst themselves, lacked the best technology, and were only recently evolved to the age of hyperspace travel."

"You're not telling me anything I don't already know!"

Quinn braced her foot, pressing against the wall for leverage, only to have Sovereign's thigh bat it aside and pin the appendage.

"I altered your original coding myself." He ensnared both wrists of the squirming woman in one strong hand, before yanking her chin up, forcing Quinn to meet his eyes. "Secretly and at great risk to the entirety of our kind. Only I knew of the time bomb I placed inside you. I had to hide it carefully, as you were so very precious and their reason for creating you so nefarious. Had the Alliance a hint, you would have been destroyed before you were old enough to defend yourself."

Quinn stilled, her muscles growing limp. Disgust bloomed on her face. "Time bomb? You did that to me? Unhinged the psionic restraint?" Voice rising, she demanded, "Do you have any idea what happens when I lose control?"

"You were never designed to have psionic abilities. While you were still in gestation, I gave you my genetic markers, placing a part of myself inside your very DNA. But your skill manifested far more aggressively and at a much earlier age than anticipated. You were only a child when you brought down the compound in a rage."

Her brows drew tight. "They were hurting my mother."

The tip of his finger followed her jaw, Sovereign studying her face as if fascinated to see it so close. "That creature only served as the vessel you were grown in. You shared no genetics with it."

Pounding her skull against the wall in an attempt to get his touch off her skin, Quinn snarled, "I know what she was! I could hear her. *The creature*, as you called her, was aware of EVERYTHING. She was aware of me!"

The smug expression fell from the looming male's face. His eyes grew dark, calculating, as understanding dawned. "You're an empath... that is how you've sensed our proximity, how you evade. But it shouldn't be possible. I know your coding by heart. You have very little Kilactarin DNA. Not enough for such a gift to foster and for you to still maintain the appearance of a human."

Violet eyes began to dilate, focused obsessively on the pulse of his carotid artery and the single drop of blood drying on his neck.

Sucking her lower lip into her mouth, Quinn imagined the taste should she stretch a bit higher and use her teeth to rip open that throat. "*You* are the reason I struggle. If I were to kill you, it would be over, and your foolish little empire of sheep, the way you eat up the universe, would end."

Sculpted lips in an archangel's face curved into a very hungry smile. "Sheep?"

Swallowing, Quinn muttered, "You became free when I tore Condor to pieces. And what have you done with your liberation? Behaved exactly as you were designed—engaging in endless campaigns to conquer human worlds. You're still slaves to your programing. Sheep."

He pressed nearer, enjoying the way her eyelids dropped at the contact. Brushing his lips to her ear, feeling her tongue drag over the drop of his blood he'd spilt to tempt her, Sovereign whispered, "You know nothing of what you are. The indoctrination by your handlers, it confused you... *lost lamb*."

At the sweet coppery taste, addiction dragged her deeper. Lips parted, forming words against his throat as if each one gave her pleasure. "You should run. But, I will chase you, I will catch you, and you will die."

Sovereign's composed calculation returned. An authoritative, chilling voice chiding, "I have seen the aftermath when you lose control, precious Sigil—

Condor, the prison colony on the moon of Vector, the rotting fleet lingering in the Durazgabi system." He avowed, "I will not allow it again."

"Allow?" He thought to command her? No one commanded her. No one was stronger, not even massive Que. A snap and furious psionics began to accumulate, little lines of energy jumping from her skin into the fool who thought to corner her, who'd had his chance to end it all yet wasted time speaking nonsense. Dyed lavender eyes sharpened. Quinn loudly cracked her neck, and forced the larger opponent away with such pleasing strength. "Allow me, sheep?"

A very male, very pleased growl filled the air when she broke his hold.

Already imagining the music of Sovereign's bones snapping, saturating herself in the compulsion, she twisted her posture into that of a born soldier. It was not hard to strike him. Her speed superior, each blow incredibly fulfilling as she toyed with her food. They were in a tangle of movements, their styles of aggression vastly different. Where Sovereign was elegant, she was unpolished, rough, and brutal. One kick and she'd shattered her table. A dodged punch dented the corroded wall. The more damage she created, the greater her need to annihilate grew. Between them, the room fell into shambles, furniture breaking, treasured baubles falling, crushed underfoot.

It wasn't long before Quinn had him on his back, his larger body under her control. Braced over Sovereign, practically drooling, she licked her lips and moved to snatch his pretty eye straight from his pretty skull.

She struck.

Everything went wrong.

There was pain and a blur as her center of gravity shifted. The grate floor cut into her cheek, her chest, her thigh, Sovereign pinning her belly down. Tossing back an elbow, she struck his ribs, the man hardly grunting as his teeth grazed the nape of her neck.

He bit down so hard she startled.

Gasping at the feeling of the bones in her neck shifting, Quinn found she couldn't move, only stare in horror as he crunched harder and another burst of feeling stunned her to momentary stillness.

Crying out, fighting like a wild thing, no matter how she tried, Sovereign had her caught, brutally biting the same place each time she grew too frantic. Exhaustion, the need to regroup, another sharp bite, and she yielded.

He released his jaw once she began to tremble.

"Shhhhhh." Sovereign stroked her body with the weight of his. "You do not need to be afraid."

There was a slithering brush of probing fingers between her closed thighs. Gripping the black leather of her small covering, he tore it away.

Quinn immediately grew frantic, screaming outrage, and the teeth returned.

Again she was forced into unnatural immobility.

A long lick over the bloody skin of her neck drew out her shiver and the haunting rumble of approval from the male. "It's time for you to submit to your consort."

Unsure how he managed to hold her down yet still slip the tips of his fingers up to trace her slit, the woman hissed, bristling at his reverberating growl when Sovereign found her clit engorged.

"You are aroused for me." With that final statement, he forced his fingers into a slippery cunt.

She instinctively squeezed around the intrusion, confused, fighting an unsettling urge to press back against thrusting digits.

Wriggling, struggling for breath, Quinn demanded, "Stop!"

Those unwelcome fingers found her piercing. Tugging and playing with it, he drew out shrill bursts of friction each time the metal skated across the sensitive nub of flesh it decorated.

Shrieking, she tried to shift his weight again.

"Surrender." Sovereign spoke as if licking her blood from his lips. "Or I will be forced to impose submission the entire time I fuck you."

"Get off—" She gave out a grunt, her words lost in her throat once his bite reestablished.

She felt his hand leave her and work the fastenings of his clothes. Before she could overcome the momentary listlessness, an unwelcome girth breached. His penetration pushed forward mercilessly until the bastard was fully sheathed.

Balls deep, Sovereign offered an extended groan so obscene her body responded, gripping tight around the intrusion and wetting him further.

Warm breath tickled over her ear. "Perfect."

When he began to thrust, Quinn struggled, gaining nothing. His answer was to display further aggression, grinding her painfully into the grate floor, moaning each time he manipulated her reaction until her cunt seeped and her insides tried to pull him in.

Smashed under the onslaught of remorseless pounding hips, Quinn wriggled, hissed, her noises twisting into calls that shamed her. Each time she keened at the fingers playing with her piercing and the fullness of his cock, he praised her—licking the bite wounds, moving with the speed and ferocity of a male giving what a raging female desired.

A teetering climax, one she had been holding back from the first intrusion, became a nightmarish thing. The leaking psionics, the fear of herself, brought her to whine, "Please…"

"Yes, Sigil." Sovereign surged, fucking in so hard she grunted at each thrust. "Beg me for more."

Saturated in stimulus, panting, pleading for a thing partway between mercy and annihilation, she screamed, "Please!" choked on the word, and climaxed so hard the world went black.

Behind her, Sovereign's jaw unhinged, the man shouting as he came.

He bit her neck one final time, erratically thrusting those last messy plunges. A long low whimper—half panicked and half gratified—hummed past parted lips once she felt him gush. Sovereign filled her to the brim, pressed tight to cork every drop of splashing ejaculate spilled in her tender passage.

Scraped raw, confused, the back of her neck a pulsing mush of torn bleeding flesh, Quinn began to weep.

"Oh, Sigil." Sovereign slid his lips over her ear. "It had to happen this way. Can you not already feel me working inside you, undoing the damage? Does it not satisfy to be mounted by your own kind? Every time we mate, you'll know completion. You'll chemically recognize your place, until you are healed of the poison they inflicted on you to punish me."

Ashamed the enemy was witnessing her weakness, Quinn turned her face away. Cheek bleeding from the rough edges of the grated floor, she welcomed the pain and stink of blood. Anything to distract from the fact he had played with her as a cat plays with a mouse—the plan of fucking her his endgame from the moment she'd stepped foot into the room.

She'd lost, he'd shamed her, and even in the moment, she could feel his come inside her womb pooling warm and unnatural.

She tried to shift her hips away from the thick plug still pulsing inside her. She tried to force that heat out.

"Hold it all, precious one," Sovereign warned, his grip growing tight again. "Hold every drop I gave you. Your body must absorb and recognize my mark if we are to break your compulsion."

She was in shock—shivering, hyperventilating, and afraid of the monster on her back.

"Please…" The word was a long entreated sob for freedom.

"You are beautiful, even when you cry." A large hand slipped under her skull to cradle it, preventing the woman from gouging her bleeding face against the abrasive floor. "It pains me our first coupling has upset you." Thumb brushing her lips like a kiss, he promised, "In time, you will learn you need not fear me."

But she was terrified.

More tears began to flow.

Quinn bawled, teeth chattering, the bastard's encouragements only upsetting her further. When she squirmed, body going numb from the pressure of the grate and the burdensome weight of the man, his organ pulsed back to life.

She froze, petrified of her body's reaction, of the blood she could feel pumping to engorge her sex further, of the slippery offered fluid which eased his passage and enticed further fucking.

Sovereign thrust gently, Quinn's hiccupping sobs twisting into soul wrenching whimpers at the decadent swirl of hips and softer scrape of teeth along her spine. He held her down as he had the first time, though she did not fight him—the second claiming infinitely tender, debilitating.

Calloused hands stroked to erase the horror, to foster nonexistent comfort.

With her eyes screwed shut, her head resting in his palm, Quinn lost the final trace of bloodlust.

Praise was lavished upon her for submission, a tongue tracing the shape of her ear when she arched her pelvis encouraging him to rut. She came screaming the name of her oldest enemy, her body greedily draining him of seed—no orgasm in her history as obliterating, as gratifying, as those desolate moments under Sovereign.

A throbbing cock emptied, splashing more fluid against her womb.

With labored breath, he commanded, "Sleep."

The effect was almost instant, and before she could reflect on why, she obeyed.

Chapter 6

The shock of waking set Quinn's heart pumping, thuds of rushing blood drowning out the ambient sounds of the room. Panic was a thing so long forgotten she hardly understood the sensation.

Sucking in a shaky breath, she registered that no male weighed her down. The grate floor wasn't cutting into her skin. Sovereign's callused hands were not stroking her as if they were familiar.

He was gone and she was alone in her bed.

But not in the room.

Puffy eyes shut tight, Quinn felt the thrum of five separate minds—all focused, all devout, all dangerous.

There was no time she could recall where ingrained impulse hadn't sent her into a frenzy at the nearness of a remnant of Project Cataclysm. Yet now there was no bloodlust, no fortifying need to rampage. The thing she hated most about herself was gone, and where it should have been, lay only cold clarity.

It was terrifying.

Motionless, she could feel blood crusting her pulped nape, the minor sting of abrasions where the grate floor had cut her flesh—a signal her sleep had been painfully short. With her genetics, physical wounds would fade completely in a matter of hours.

It was her insides she feared would remain altered.

The urge to shrink deeper into the bedding like a frightened child brought bile to her mouth.

That would not do.

The salty fan of lashes rose in a measured sweep. Five Imperial soldiers stood at attention. Only the largest dared to look at her. The male preened, eyes glowing against an impassive expression.

Though he did not wear the armor of his order, woven into his long white shock of hair were the small metal disks of a highly ranked warrior. One of the most recognizable tyrants in the known universe, Karhl—Lord Commander of the Empire, and one of the most powerful Brothers to Sovereign—stood in her cramped room.

Having him for a warden... was bad.

"Do you feel violent?" Karhl's voice was oddly deep, similar to Que's robotic vibration.

Quinn blinked, the image of the male somewhat obscured by her hair. "And if I should say yes, you are to subdue me?"

He answered at once, head bowing fractionally. "It would be my honor."

Gentle tone or no, the implication was not missed.

Fear fresh, she imagined he too would mount her as Sovereign had, with four converts serving as living restraints—one for each of her limbs—so the Lord Commander might do his work and fill her with the same chemical soup Sovereign claimed was her salvation.

Paranoid, red-rimmed eyes reassessed what her brain had calculated from the first moments she'd returned to consciousness: she was outnumbered and ignorant of just how complex her entrapment was.

"You remain distressed," Karhl spoke again, drawing her attention back to his beautiful stone-carved face. "How may I soothe you?"

The atrocities she'd committed were nothing compared to what the Lord Commander had inflicted on planet after planet. The man had destroyed whole human populations, committed acts of genocide against billions unwilling to convert. The knowledge didn't stop her from hissing, "You could get out."

"I cannot."

Eyeballing the intruder, Quinn sat up, the fallen bed sheet exposing breasts still wrapped in the binding she'd performed in the night before. Unsure fingers traced over her damaged cheek while she tried to ignore the slippery excess of Sovereign's sperm leaking from her body to wet the mattress.

Observing her every breath, Karhl spoke. "It was decided decades ago, amongst the greatest of us, that force would be an unfortunate necessity."

At the giant's words, Quinn turned her aching neck so she might glare and let out a threatening growl.

Karhl met her gaze, undaunted, and continued speaking in that flat, dull tone. "We have conquered worlds full of pleasures to tempt you to us. You resisted. We sent dignitaries across the universe; you fled from your family. Aware of your reasons, we worried for you, young one. Trackers, bounty hunters, all avenues were explored. It has been a century of alternate efforts with no result. Your rape… there was no other way to assure progress."

The kind of rape where the attacker forces pleasure so burdensome it stings worse than the humiliation of defeat.

Lip trembling, Quinn clenched her jaw, choosing to stare at the wall when she found she could no longer look at the male. "I am surprised you are not trying to find a nicer word to justify *progress*."

"As it evolved, did you not enjoy him? Several of your acquired former sexual partners claimed you preferred intense aggression."

That statement was incredibly unsettling.

The pleasure had been compulsory. A base piece of her had reveled in it; a greater part had hated it. And the giant Lord Commander, with his piercing eyes and fair color, was aware. He'd been nearby throughout the entire coupling. Had her mind not been so distorted, so enamored with her ultimate prey, she would have recognized it then. "Did you enjoy the show?"

"I witnessed your liberation. I watched over you, ready to intervene if it was necessary." No judgment sat in sea glass eyes, only pride directed at her. "You are powerful. Sovereign was almost unable to subdue you himself."

When the compliment did nothing but earn him a scathing look, he rationalized, steady and unaffected. "You remain overwhelmed and understandably conflicted."

The Irdesian Empire was very powerful, they were on Pax, the byway was closed, and her greatest enemy implied something she could hardly bear to think of. "Do not presume to know me, *Lord Commander*."

Striking, large, and closing in, Karhl said, "I watched you rip a massive reinforced wall out of the ground with your psionics at Condor. You then threw it at a wave of Alliance soldiers, killing them all. Having just taken a bullet for you, I reached out to touch your shoulder, to help you. You threw me farther than the wall." The frightening soldier—one who had lived centuries longer than she, who had fought the war against the Alliance and formed the Empire—stepped closer and put a hand where he'd tried to touch the child long ago. Thumb grazing her slave collar he asked, "Are you going to throw me again for trying to help you, Sigil?" Thick fingers curled under the too tight contraption and Karhl crushed the device. "Sovereign removed your true collar when he shattered your conditioned compulsion." The crumbling metal scraps dropped bit by bit to land in her lap. "He did what needed to be done so you might understand your place in the universe."

Even as he spoke, warm hands capable of causing her great harm circled where the collar had reassuringly squeezed for the last decade.

Quinn's hand flew up to grip his wrist, wrenching it, and finding fulfillment in the grind of his bone. "Breaking my collar will summon Pax overseers."

Ignoring the discomfort, Karhl worked the pads of his fingers over the flaking scabs on her nape. Soft feeling wormed against tender skin. Violent thoughts muted. Quinn's heart rate decreased.

He spoke, "There is no angle we have not considered. You are blanketed by the Empire and safe here."

She knew better. No one was safe on Pax.

"I will not hurt you." Karhl's instant pinch between her vertebrae fostered a shuddering impulse of pleasure down in her belly, a dim echo of the almost orgasmic power that had left Quinn stunned when Sovereign bit her the night before.

She blinked, and liquid fell over the sticky abrasions on her cheek.

Nothing made sense. All the running, all the years believing one thing and fearing only herself, when all along she should have greatly feared them. Wet eyes looked up at a monster she'd been created to destroy. "I don't understand."

"You were designed so light pressure between shifted cervical vertebrae three and four would induce calm. A Kilactarin trait highlighted with Sudenovan matriarch." Karhl offered a deep mechanical hum. "Allow me to comfort you."

Her hand shot up to shield the vulnerable spot. The Lord Commander acquiesced.

Without the pressure from his fingers, Quinn's stupor faded. Anger replaced it. "The bastard gnawed my neck bloody."

She could sense Karhl's feelings were resolved, the man certain all had been done as it should have been. "A bite heightens arousal and subdues defense in an aggressive female. It was done out of mercy. He did not wish to give you only fear and pain."

Sovereign's mercilessness was legendary. To hear him spoken of in any other way was iniquitous.

Quinn edged out of the Lord Commander's reach, placing the bed as a barrier between them. Upon standing, her thighs grew wet with more of Sovereign's leaking mark, Karhl glancing down to view the shine of semen dripping down pale flesh. Had the emotions she sensed in him been reflected on his face, the warrior would have been smiling. But he didn't. Karhl was expressionless, very Axirlan in his makeup, similar to her Que in all the wrong ways.

Those humans with him were also unordinary, a caliber of convert Quinn had not been exposed to before. They had been altered, as if she could smell the Lord Commander's contamination upon them.

"These are my chosen elite," Karhl answered upon viewing the scrutiny of his men. "A highly coveted rank few survive advanced levels of conversion to attain."

Hybrids? A dim reflection of the one they'd been altered to mimic. She edged further from Karhl and nearer to the closest soldier, finding limpid blue competing with the natural brown of the human's eyes. It was more than brainwashing. The man had been altered on a cellular level.

Karhl's face remained impassive. "Human populations have been domesticated."

Quinn shot a nasty look at the man seeking to educate her. "Conversion or death? You wish for them to mimic you as if you're superior? You are all far more greedy and violent than they ever were."

"Control was taken so strays might be advanced properly and renegades removed. Conversion progresses us all."

"And who are you to decide the direction of their evolution? You would kill off an entire species to create something to use." Frowning, Quinn turned back to the soldier, seeing the convert refused to meet her eye. "As we were used."

"The Alliance would have stopped at nothing to hunt you, Sigil. Any cost; any loss of life. Whole planets would have been burned to ash if even a *suggestion* you might walk its crust had been made. Do not condemn us when your Brothers have always offered feral humans a choice over annihilation. How else were you to survive?"

Pressure built behind her eyes, the human soldier's face wavered in her field of vision. Taking in the profile of what was still a young man, Quinn whispered, "Do you hear what he says? They would blame me for what's been done to you?"

There was no reply.

Quinn snarled. "Look at me!"

Karhl approached to stand behind her, his hand hovering over her shoulder as she stared at his underling, utterly distraught. "He is forbidden to do such a thing."

She pleaded, unsure why the soldier didn't understand he'd been mutilated. "Look at me."

"You greatly outrank him, but Sovereign has overruled you here."

And there it was. Sovereign—everything boiled down to Sovereign. His very existence controlled her life no matter how far she'd run.

"I refuse to be blamed for the state of human affairs. I cannot help what I am, and want nothing to do with your empire. I never did. I *tried* to leave you in peace. The same respect was not extended in reciprocation."

Karhl's hand descended the final distance to softly pet a female who was confused, angry, and unwell.

His eyes roamed over her body, lingering on the swell of muscled thigh and hip, the dip of her belly, and upon breasts hardly covered by pleasure slave's garb. "You are a fully grown woman now, Sigil, with wisdom to temper your impulses. But you are still controlled by them through no fault of your own." He delivered cold truth unflinchingly. "Understand that the noticeable effects of your mating will not last. This uncertain freedom from your compulsion to kill us will return without further measures. With us, your family, so near and escape routes closed, how long do you really think you could resist your programming?" All traces of gentleness drained from his quasi-Axirlan face, Karhl growling just enough to earn her focused attention. "Unless you submit, you will attack, and he will force you again. It cannot be helped."

Unsure which unsettled her more, the sense of devotion from the Lord Commander or the fear the compulsion might return after a short terrifying moment of freedom, Quinn said, "You think I don't recognize the manipulation at work here? Sovereign is conveniently gone. A Lord Commander stands in his place so I might be calm and measured... *converted* before rage sets in for what was done and I kill us all."

"Your judgment is partially correct. But I assure you, young one, my goal is not manipulation, but pure assessment. It is my duty to confirm the compulsion was successfully muted. The proximity of Sovereign, and your reaction upon waking near the one who'd hurt you may have unbalanced my evaluation." Without hesitation, he admitted, "I also desired to have you to myself so that I might be the one to tend you. I wish to offer comfort you would not allow were he here."

His tone of voice was so like Que's she unwillingly responded to it, silently acceding, fully aware Karhl was not her companion.

"I have bled for you. Personally sought you in every corner of the galaxy." The Lord Commander was absolutely sincere. "Since your creation, each life I have claimed I took in your name."

The calm induced by his voice vanished, and she found the will to look back at the man. Everything in her expression spoke of hate.

Nervously licking her lower lip, she began edging towards the lavatory and away from the beautiful male with his oddness and unwelcome devotion. "I could kill your four *elite* soldiers so fast I doubt the last could draw before I shattered his spine. But you... you frighten me, and I cannot help but wonder if that was the very reason you were chosen." Violence would not set her free, nor could she negotiate with his level of zealotry. "I must say his plan was well-enacted."

"My intention is not to frighten you. Once you are home and settled, you will find peace as Imperial Consort in our care. All this will seem as nothing."

Quinn moved a step closer the lavatory. "As a prisoner."

Karhl offered a nod. "Though I would prefer you viewed the arrangement differently, you are essentially correct." He gestured for her to enter the target of her evasion and see to her body's needs. "But your freedoms will increase as your healing progresses."

"How do you not understand? I was designed so Sovereign would desire me. That does not mean he should. I hate you all, yet never killed one of you."

Karhl followed her step for step. "Fifty-seven of your Brothers sacrificed their lives in search of you. Some you damaged. And you have killed three."

She had not known that. "Not on purpose! I don't want to kill you. Every day I fight the impulse to carry out the assignment I was created for. I just want to *be*. But you keep coming, and some days I can't stop."

"We know."

His calm infuriated her. "I have not slipped in thirty years. I have not told anyone what you are."

"What *we* are, Sigil."

She closed her eyes, feeling anger heat her face. "I am not a sheep."

"Bathe as you desire." Karhl gestured towards the wash cubicle.

More than anything, Quinn wanted Sovereign's stink off of her... even if that required an audience.

When she stripped the sad remnants of her clothes, the looming Lord Commander did not avert his eyes. He set his gaze to each uncovered bit of skin, and she felt as if he was mentally licking his lips, no matter his stoic persona.

Never taking her eye from the invader, scrubbing until her flesh was raw, Quinn sought comfort in the knowledge that under the feet of her one-man audience was a grate which could be lifted—a passage she'd carved through air ducts, drainage, and metal sheeting beneath it.

One way or another, she was getting out of this room. She'd just need to bide her time.

The preset timer ended, the chemical cleansing spray stopped, and Karhl offered her a length of towel. "Everything you require during the remainder of our tenure in this domicile has been provided, including appropriate clothing." At the flick of his fingers one of the soldiers brought forth a quantity of fabric and handed it to the large Lord Commander.

Quinn looked down at the beaded red silk, similar in shade to the length of streaming fabric she twisted in at Swelter, and found no pleasure in its beauty.

Brushing past him, she moved to her cabinets to choose from familiar things.

Karhl moved nearer. "Slaves' garb is not appropriate for the Imperial Consort. Please wear the dress."

Her arms went through a length of worn robe Que had brought her from a Tessan outer world decades before. Sash knotted with an angry yank, she refused, and walked from the bedroom in search of food.

Frozen at the gateway that overlooked her quarter's only other room, Quinn found the wreckage and ruin had been cleaned sometime in her sleep.

Her broken treasures were gone, erased. Her blood no longer stained the grates.

Chewing a bit of torn skin near her nail, Quinn felt the weight of a hand settle on her shoulder again and flinched, unaware she stared at the spot where she had been held facedown to the floor.

A large thumb skimmed her nape.

That was all it took for Quinn to double over, vomiting all over the floor.

Swept up before she caught her breath, she found herself rushed back to the lavatory, her wet hair held back in the hands of her new keeper as the rest of her stomach contents splattered against the basin.

Childhood years of torture she'd survived with more grace: electro shock training, bone breaking strikes from combat instructors who hit her as if she'd been full-grown, poisons injected daily to test tolerance and increase immunity... yet she disgraced herself while one of the most feared warriors in the Empire tended to her like the child he inferred she was.

The bed came soft under her back, Karhl covering her body with blankets as he spoke. "Sovereign has been summoned. He will be here shortly."

She couldn't see past the dark spots in her vision, curled up as the Lord Commander kneaded her nape. Then another was touching her, enveloping her in muscled limbs, in warmth. Lips pressed against her temple, soft words were whispered in her ear, and the oblivion of unconsciousness arrived.

The next time she woke, she was dressed in the layered beauty of the beaded red silk.

Chapter 7

Surrounded by the scent of falling rain, Quinn smiled, breathing in time to the heartbeat under her ear. "How many years did I sleep, Que?"

The thing she was cradled against stiffened.

An exhale brushed her crown, lips followed. "Not years, Sigil. Half a cycle."

Drowsy eyes opened to find that in place of the snowy white bulk of her friend, tan sinew was pressed to her cheek. Sovereign's bared chest served as her pillow, his jacket open, the skin to skin contact warm. Yet the rest of him was fully clothed—as was she.

Confined in the red gown, too much fabric twisted about her, both draping and tight. Nudity would have been preferable. So much clothing altered the paradigm.

Her life in Pax was lived nearly naked. That was her normal. That gave her power.

Foreign, restricting clothes pinched and changed her purpose from invisible pleasure slave to… something unspeakable.

Quinn drew in a deep breath and found the man's scent—just like the fingers manipulating the nerves in her nape—equally distressing and sedating. Sovereign's touch and his physiology had a chemical effect, manipulating her into a state of unnatural calm with little effort.

The hand by her cheek curled, Quinn's nails burrowing between bared ribs until they drew blood.

Sovereign allowed it.

When her fingertips were coated in little beads of red, Quinn found it pretty, running the fluid from fingernail to tongue, unsure why she did such a thing or why the action earned Sovereign's rumbled hum of approval.

She had intended to annoy him, not please him.

No longer toying with the drips of blood, her eyes left his torso. The Imperial soldiers still haunted her room, Karhl watching her as he had before.

A finger caught under her chin, Sovereign turning Quinn's frowning face up so no other but him was in her view. The man, it would seem, didn't want to share her attention. "Why would you sleep for years, Sigil?"

Brows drawing tight, Quinn refused to answer.

The pressure of Sovereign's mouth descended upon hers. He breathed between her lips, punishing her silence and adding his taste on her tongue as retribution.

Smoothing her hair, breathing in her impatient exhale, he held the agitated female and demanded, "Answer me."

The second he began to seek another kiss, she acquiesced. "Que places me in cryo when I find I can no longer resist the urge to... do things,"

Soft words tempted further explanation. "To prevent you from coming to me?"

A strange cloying comfort came with the memory of just what *things* she'd done. "Sometimes I fall asleep and cannot be woken. Sometimes he needed to prevent me from slaughtering everything between me and the meat I wish to gnaw off your bones."

Every last tick of excitement growing on Quinn's face was there for Sovereign to see. Her breath grew excited and even a hint of a smile played at her lips.

"How many years have you slept in total?"

Licking the sharp edges of her teeth, Quinn practically purred. "Decades. I have slept decades so you could live."

The subtle shift in his expression altered from enticement to irritation. "How very generous the Axirlan was to steal that time from you."

No one slandered her friend and lived.

Quinn grew nasty. "I should have killed you on Condor. I should have dug through the rubble until I found you and ripped out your heart with my teeth!"

A sharp pinch came to her neck, Sovereign silently warning that he would induce total submission should she lose her temper further.

Furious, Quinn unwillingly wilted. But her eyes warned that if she could strike him in that moment, she would.

The bastard dared to kiss the tip of her nose.

When the threat of his fingers on her nape disappeared, her audible breath—a rattling growl—warned him she was nowhere near calm. Sovereign traced her angry flush with the back of his knuckles, dug his fingertips into her hair to work them against her scalp in a more conventional effort to soothe. "There is no more war for you to fight. You may be angry, but you've lost nothing of your honor by my methods."

"I can almost hear Commander Dimitri when you say, 'honor, methods'. It seems something he would spout while he had me tortured, vids of you fucking courtesans playing on every wall. I remember one female in particular. Her hair was blonde and she had pretty eyes like you do. I have seen you come in her, over, and over, and over. Dimitri enjoyed drowning and resuscitating me to that common performance. Every time you fucked her, I enjoyed the pain of stagnant water pooling in my lungs. There was a brunette too. They only burned me when you mounted her. I used to pray you would. But, you had such a thing for that blonde."

An angry throat noise and Sovereign's seeming sweetness was immediately ruined by naked malice. "Beloved, had I known—"

"You would have chosen the brunette?" Quinn laughed. It was a mean sound, an unforgiving one. "Only one creature has ever helped me. He has done more for me than I will ever be able to repay, and if I found out you've hurt him, your death would be slow and painful."

Sovereign schooled his features back into affability, brushing his lips over hers in a murmured, "Harming the Axirlan would be counterproductive to my goal." The backs of his fingers ghosted over her cheek again, a tender gesture that did not match the growing violence in Sovereign's eyes. "You are separated from his influence. He cannot reach you. Show me that you are willing, give me no cause to be threatened, and the alien's free existence will continue."

Caught in those eyes, tossed between the worming desire to let go of control and strike him down, or make a run for her escape hatch, she hissed, "If you *ever* hurt him, I will rip you and all your kind apart. Every last sheep will die."

Sovereign's answer was paired with a slow stroke down her flank. "Then understand my position. If you seek him, think to hide from me behind your *pet*, I will kill him. The Axirlan has no place in your life."

She could sense he meant his threat as much as she did hers. It was an impasse. But, they both knew if she challenged him in that moment, tangled in red silk and strong limbs, she would lose.

Before she might formulate a response, a corded arm urged her to lie back. His lips began to taste her throat. "Promise me you'll let him go and all this talk of killing can be over."

That would never happen. Ever.

She tried to push him off, it made no difference. Attention was lavished along her jaw, the fragile lobe of her ear, Sovereign fitting his body to hers as he muttered, "I do not mean to be harsh with you, Sigil. Understand, I speak, and will act, out of jealousy and anger at his part in keeping you from me. Had he not interfered and stolen years of your life, it would have saved you decades of suffering. I have a considerable need to punish him that I will ignore."

"His restraint made it so I could not hunt you, gut you, and eat what I found inside. You should thank him." Quinn was caught, gasping and hating any sensation her enemy skillfully stirred.

Sovereign chuckled. "You taste my blood and moan... growing so aroused I can smell it." He nosed her throat, smirking as he licked her precisely where she had cut him only hours ago. "The hunt... this misinterpretation you cling to in your limited knowledge of your genetics and the negative effects of your indoctrination—what you experienced, the *need*, was a precursor to your fertile cycle. You sought me to breed. I owe him no thanks for preventing such bliss."

An unintentional pop of psionics, and she threw Sovereign far enough back that she could evade his hands and unwelcome sighs.

Arms tight around her middle, she backed into a corner. The look on her face—it was if he had struck her. "I am sterile! You are wrong and you should not say such things!"

She had tried everything to conceive, to give Que what she knew he desired. How dare Sovereign say differently. How dare he come here!

How dare he touch her and lie!

Beside her in an instant, Sovereign splayed his fingers over her womb.

Bearing an expression of exultation, he claimed, "Inducing ovulation requires sharp pressure"—he brushed her tangled hair aside to press a kiss to her nape—"here, and the sperm of a genetic equivalent. Your Axirlan could never give you children as I can. Nor could he love you as I do. The species is physically incapable on both counts. Let's not pretend you do not know their laws. Were your Que to hear these things, he would give you to me willingly, *unable to regret it*, because I am best for you and will provide what is missing in your existence."

No.

It was impossible.

Quinn's attention went to Karhl, as if the large warrior might shake his head and negate such a cruel statement.

He did not. "Sovereign is correct, young one. Axirlan code would never allow him to upset the natural order, or your place in it. Que will leave you to us when the situation has been explained. There will be no resistance from his side. He will go in peace, unharmed, so long as you make a vow to forget him."

Her heart breaking, Quinn found her eyes were unable to part from the sea glass of the Lord Commander's. "Que saved my life. After Condor, I was... when he found me, I knew *nothing* of the universe but pain, survival, and rage." Sensing the deep hate both men harbored in their thoughts, she defended her only friend. "I tried to murder him, to steal his ship when my beacon drew him near. He still took me in, even though I was feral and didn't speak for years. Que is the only family I have ever known. We belong together. Harm to him would kill me!"

"I won't execute the Axirlan because I do not wish to see you saddened. I will let him walk away." The words were breathed over her clavicle, Sovereign answering her pleas where she could not see the abhorrence on his face—only feel it. "See, I can be reasonable."

The honesty she sensed enraged her. They believed this. They believed Que would leave her. They believed she would abandon him.

Bubbling rage, black as tar, flowed from her heart all the way down to her fingertips.

Why offer lies when she could hurt these invaders now? Kill Sovereign, then Karhl... the soldiers. Anyone who stood in her way on Pax, who dared to breathe her air would be next.

Violence—a grand slaughter—would be perfection.

Everyone between her and Que must die.

In her haze, Sovereign worked to draw her back to the bed, cooing and sweet as if they were lovers.

Mesmerized by thoughts of all the ways she could murder him, Quinn let her nails dip into Sovereign's open shirt.

Claws drew blood, and she moaned.

His head raised, mouth swollen from use, and those oceanic eyes met hers with no shame. "I can sense your growing bloodlust. I'd prefer not to force you to end it. Show me you will try and the issue of the Axirlan will not be spoken of again."

Biting back a vile retort, Quinn stiffened once he began bunching up the layers of the ridiculous red gown.

He pressed her back to her bed, seeking soft skin.

The sickening anticipation, the puffing juicy flesh between her legs swelling in expectation of slow encroaching fingers, drew her attention away from her hunger to slaughter.

As if he appreciated her internal war, Sovereign whispered, "You need this."

Heedless of the Lord Commander and four converts who stood in the room, Sovereign delved into her slippery folds. Tongue dipping into her mouth, it undulated in a kiss far more lecherous than any she'd known.

Que never kissed her, the act foreign to his species and one she seldom took part in with others.

To have someone do it now, to taste the man... felt forbidden. Each sweep of his tongue, stirred sensation just like the feelings he'd fostered when he'd forced her on the floor.

Hooked fingers tangled inside her pussy, a sure thumb bobbing Quinn's swollen clit. When she began to croon, her hips involuntarily rocking, Sovereign leaned back so he might watch.

Eye to eye, the beauty of her lips parted just before her core spasmed and clenched tight.

There was a problem.

Release had not calmed her hunger. Orgasm had not satisfied.

Through the blended haze of bloodlust and physical desire, she found the lesson.

Her madness was still multiplying, the impulse to hunt growing.

Physical pleasure had done nothing because Sovereign's part to play was not over. He needed to spill inside her so her body could register... what he was.

Through this manipulation, it seemed he asked permission, though he didn't ask at all.

He wanted her to believe it was her choice.

The bastard.

She knew better. So long as he had the power, he would fuck her again regardless.

She could lie pliant, or she could be pinned down.

Rolling to give him her back, she stared at the wall and sought the illusion of solitude—a moment where she might gather herself and breathe through the urge. Then she could calm down and he would not have to touch her.

She was not given the time.

Unsure if he had misread her movement as an offering, she let out a nervous squeak when his teeth found her spine.

Yet Sovereign only sucked softly and did not bite.

Hand tucked into her bodice to pluck and twist a nipple with fingers still wet with her juices, he ordered, "Trust me."

He may have asked for trust, but his movements anticipated hostility. An arm came tight around her middle so she could not pull away. Behind her, Sovereign freed his cock. Up went her skirt. Erection swollen and already dripping, his bulbous glans smeared through the slippery remains of her climax. On an exhale, he pressed forward, slithering fully into her core.

It killed her, the exuberance of her moan.

The best she could do was ignore her body, the intruders in her room, the cock slipping slowly in and out of aroused flesh, and think of nothing. That was the only way she'd live this down.

If she fought back, he'd force the point. If she participated, she'd never forgive herself.

Sovereign had other plans for the limp woman.

When she grew stiff, he pulled her upright, her back to his chest, and took her with her legs spread over his knees.

Gone were the smooth movements and gentle thrusts. Hand about her throat, and another at her breast, he braced the woman. Lips to her ears, he made sure she heard each guttural moan, each gasp he made as he drove forward.

Sadistic music to time his violence to.

Still, she tried to mentally detach.

Eyes screwed shut, fighting to escape how very devastating his possession could be, Quinn was unprepared to feel another set of lips brush hers. Startled, lashes lifted and she found Karhl had seized her mouth with an expertise that shook her. His tongue teased at her lips and the white-haired warrior stroked under her skirt to stimulate the apex of her sex.

He was sweet where Sovereign was crude.

The power in which they destroyed her resistance, pulling her between aggression and tenderness was frightening in its success. In tandem they decimated; Sovereign fucking so fast, the wet sounds of brutal thrusts were not drowned out even by her cries. Karhl's tracing the sensitive roof of Sigil's mouth while gently massaging the stiff little bundle of nerves until climax brought her to scream.

Any last trace of her growing aggression was shattered with that first splash of answering come.

Sovereign pawed over her womb, tasting the side of her neck as he continued to spill, Karhl fingering the labia stretched tight around a thick twitching cock to extend her pleasure.

With one sucking kiss to her bottom lip, the Lord Commander pulled away.

His hand trailed from under her skirt so he might answer the distressed look in her eyes. "Do not fret, young one. Sovereign holds the greatest claim, but as the only female of our species, some will see you as mother, others sister... the strongest of us will desire you as lover."

The Lord Commander's earlier possessive behavior began to make sense. Knowing it must have been sanctioned by the emperor still groaning and gushing inside her, Quinn grimaced. "I am to be shared."

There was a look of compassion in the rugged edges of Karhl's eyes. Wiping a trace of saliva from her lips, the white-haired warrior clarified, "You are the Eve of our people, Sigil. Your daughters are something we have longed for, for a century. Submit to Sovereign. Be healed, bear his offspring, and your Brothers will be well-pleased and patient to see our numbers swell."

Sovereign growled, contented, gripping Quinn's breast in the way he found made her skin bump and throat constrict. "Do not try to hide your resurfacing compulsion again. I will not allow you to suffer."

Quinn thought of the grate in the lavatory, let the thought of it dampen growing anxiety.

Sovereign was inside her far more than physically. She could feel the chemical interactions, the softening of her organs to allow him as deep as he wished to go—the minutia had been missed in her previous panic, and something about noticing it as he held and stroked her, as he whispered he adored her, left her boneless.

She didn't even try to claw her way off of him.

Staring off into space, Quinn muttered, "Que once brought me a male who looked like you, unaware of my appetite. I… did things to him. My friend couldn't stop me. Not without shooting me three times and digging a blade between my ribs. By then it was too late. It took four years in cryo for my brainwaves to normalize. When I woke, the first thing I remembered was the taste of that stranger's heart."

"What did it taste like?" Sovereign asked, kissing her damp temple, hearing her old pain.

"Bitter."

"Did you regret it?"

Sigil blinked once. The corners of her mouth turned down. "I still regret it."

Sovereign confessed his own sin. "At the birth of the Empire, I found a courtesan with hair almost the same shade as yours. I brought her to the palace, rode her day and night—made her think I cared for her, all the while imagining you. But she wasn't you." Sovereign's hands toyed with a length of plum stained waves, eyeing the altered color with distaste. "I grew bored and cast her off. She killed herself."

At the birth of the Empire, Sigil had still been only a child. "I suppose we're both monsters."

Black hair hung in his eyes as he turned her chin to taste her mouth. "At least I didn't try to eat her, *lost lamb*."

Chapter 8

She'd been fed, the human soldiers having dug through her supplies to create a plate, offering it as if it was theirs to give. Sovereign had not left her to Karhl. Instead he remained, watching her every move as if calculating her thoughts.

But he was not an empath.

Even so, she looked so worried Sovereign did not need to be. It was in the way she fingered the almost healed scabs at her nape and kept to the corner furthest from her guard. Fidgeting with the dress kept her hands busy, for it was tight, cumbersome with all its layers—designed, she imagined, to slow her into stuttering steps.

Sovereign offered her a book, an actual book with pages discolored by time and use. It was such an odd thing to see, her fingers could not help but reach for it. The old-Earth artifact was fascinating, had a scent to it that was both dusty and appealing. Finding a place to sit, her back to the wall so, should one of the unwelcome males in the room move, she would know, Quinn opened the cover.

She read through the tome quickly, familiar with the language but unaccustomed to such a collection of stories. Unsure if she misunderstood, she read it again. Her eyes broke from the page, the frown returning.

"The book did not please you?" Sovereign was staring at her, assessing.

"The concept is unusual. This bible is full of violence and contradictions: a vengeful god, the pacifist, accepting messiah whose friends used his resurrection to further their agendas and influence. They were obviously lying. Humans are power hungry and can never be trusted."

"Those humans do not exist anymore."

Her eyes went to the soldiers, the changed beings that even after modification were a far cry from her genetics. "There are still free humans. I have seen their societies."

There was no judgment, only curiosity when Sovereign asked, "And they cast you out?"

"No." There was no need to say more, Quinn's interactions with humans had not gone well, but they'd never cast her out.

Sovereign understood the silence. "They hurt you."

"In the same way you just did."

She could see it on his face, the misunderstanding evolve to abject fury. Quinn knew what had crossed his mind. Only her wounded child form would have been weak enough for a human to harm.

He hid the rage, and asked gently, "These humans, where are they?"

"Long since digested," Quinn answered, looking to frighten the man.

Sovereign took a step closer, his voice infinitely soft. "Why did you eat them?"

Quinn reply was as icy as her eyes. "I was starving."

"And when the humans were gone?"

Bored, Quinn sighed. "I was alone on a planet where the flora made me vomit and the fauna took more skill to catch than a person."

"This world you lived on..." Sovereign kneeled, his fingertips landing lightly on Quinn's knees. "You built yourself a throne, you played queen?"

She had done that with supply crates at the vacant brigand outpost, made a court of skeletons to talk to. Sovereign must have been there. He had found that wild place.

"I was just a child." She grew defensive. "Children play."

"But you were never allowed to play." A dark light in his eyes, and the man shared another bit of her private history. "A nurse once gave you a toy in secret. They made you kill her when the doll was discovered."

No, he was wrong. Breaking the nurse's neck had been mercy. Her handlers were torturing the woman, peeling off her skin. "I killed her because I wanted to."

"And the doll?"

There was no reason to think on old things. "I do not want to talk anymore."

"Are you afraid of Condor?"

A wicked smirk graced her mouth. "Who fears a pile of ashes?"

"But you did not burn it down." Sovereign shook his head. "Your Brothers found old records, recordings, the notes of your handlers. I watched what was done to you, what made you this way."

Being accused of being *a way* did not please her.

Sovereign continued. "I am the one who burned Condor to the ground. And then I hunted and tortured every last human who'd survived your attack. Even their descendants were punished. We removed the Alliance from power, scoured planets clean of their infection. They were made to pay for what was done."

She turned her head away.

"Sigil, they thought we were unaware of your existence. That day in the hall, that chance meeting, we had planned for *years*." Sovereign stroked his hand down her legs, running his palms over the fabric bunched at her calves. "Just seeing you once was worth the punishment."

"Did they take away your toy too?" She mocked, alluding to the blonde he'd fucked almost daily.

"They killed twenty of my dearest Brothers, cut out my tongue, a testicle, broke every bone in my body."

Quinn was not impressed. "We regenerate."

Solemn, he nodded. "*We* do. But unlike the mythology you just read, those we love do not come back to life."

She couldn't help herself, or mitigate the venom in her response. "I love only Que."

Male hands fisted the fabric of her skirt in a solid grip.

Quinn imagined all the thoughts running through his mind to make his emotions so volatile yet keep his face so still. Those pretty eyes seemed tranquil, the only tension in the man his grip on her skirt.

She matched her breath and heartbeat to his, ready to strike if he so much as tried to lift her skirt.

Still, he only stared as if silently reminding her that aggression would end badly. She was outnumbered, trapped in a corner.

She would lose.

Sovereign mirrored her exhalation.

Quinn spoke to herself, unsure how everything had gone so wrong. The entire scenario made no sense. "I was created to kill you."

"You were created"—he released her skirt, turned his fingers, and skimmed her palm—"to disarm me. You were fashioned as the only viable female so that we could not strike you back. You were brainwashed to hate me, even though your very genetics partner mine." Sovereign eased close as he tried to seduce. "You do not need to be scared of me.

In my care, there won't be punishments or torture. All I offer you can keep."

"So long as I stay in this room or one like it?"

"You are restless, I understand." Toying with her fingers, interlacing her smaller bones with his, Sovereign smiled. "Pax is no worthy place for you. Soon we will leave."

But the stillness of the station, the silence, let her know the byway remained offline. With no sound of combat in the levels around her, there could be no coup. Drinta was still preparing for something. If Quinn was correct, the bitch-queen lacked the knowledge that Sovereign already walked the halls of her kingdom.

All that had been done—the collection of warriors, shutting down the byway—was done for the Herald's eyes. If Drinta really thought the Irdesian Emperor was there, there would be no peace, no silence. Probabilities began to align, Quinn sitting silent while Sovereign kneeled before her and toyed with her fingers.

"There are jungles, Sigil, full of trees and wildlife you could only imagine, sanctioned for you to play in—beaches, mountains, palaces far superior to this mold-ridden wreck. Worlds are waiting for you." Sovereign purred, working to entice her interest. "Let these things, this shadow life, go."

It was offspring he needed, even Karhl had confirmed it. "Advancing our species, that is why you say these things. You have no choice in the matter. Otherwise you would not want me."

"Such a thought makes you unhappy." Sovereign understood, knowing the majority of her life she'd been used in one way or another. "Our daughters will be adored, but never as much as I worship their mother. But it is true. I cannot help but love you."

With so much diplomacy, such slippery compliments, Quinn sneered. "You should have been a Herald."

He eased closer, his fingers gliding over her inner wrist. "It seems so long as I am on my knees, you speak. Is that a game you wish to play, diplomat and queen? I can offer negotiation. You can take what you wish."

The emperor *was* less intimidating kneeling, his position purposefully putting him at a disadvantage. But with the Lord Commander looking on—in view of four converts—Sovereign's disadvantage would not last long.

Quinn frowned.

Time on Pax was precious, the station known to her—the tunnels, the crawlspaces. If Sovereign dragged her to the Empire, escape would be almost impossible. But when she fled, what of the Tessan boy? His cryotube would lay forgotten until the battery cell ran dry. He would die after decades of sleep, or be ejected into space to wake scared and without air.

She needed to open the fucking byway and get him off the station.

A heavy hand came to rest on her shoulder. It was not Sovereign's. Snapping her eyes to Karhl, Sigil froze as the kneading began. "Calm yourself, young one. Your heart is beating too fast."

It seemed they all had their special skills.

Her liabilities had increased with remembrance of the hidden child. She had an obligation to the boy, had to open the byway, had to find Que. It was beginning to feel impossible. "It is difficult to be calm when surrounded by the enemy."

The white-haired Lord Commander cupped her cheek, promising, "You won't always think of us that way."

"So you say. In this moment, I feel as if you've stolen my world from me."

Sovereign smiled, he pressed a kiss to her hands. "I will replace it with a better world."

A better world? There was nothing better than the squalor of Pax. With a sigh, Quinn asked, "Do you have any other books I can read?"

In fact, Sovereign did. He handed it over and left her in peace.

Hours passed, she seemed content, and when she slipped towards the lavatory, neither man followed, no soldier was sent to observe her tend her body, and it was several minutes before a blast sent the ground off balance.

The door was forced open with a burst of violent psionics.

Sovereign found the space vacant, smoke rising up from the grate floor.

She was gone.

※

The station, her playground, offered so many crevices where she might hide. Scuttling about from deck to deck, never lingering in one place long, offered assurances Sovereign would not find her. But that was not the art of a true survivor, nor would time allow such comforts as the dank dark. She had less than a cycle before the urge might claim her and drag her right back to him. Therefore, progress had to be aggressive.

Hiding was out of the question.

She had to save the Tessan boy. She had to convince Drinta to reopen the Byway. And she had to get to Que so he might save her from herself before Sovereign's mark wore off.

Stirring up the hive, sparking the powder keg, walking right up to Drinta's balcony to sit with the bitch-queen—Sovereign would never anticipate such a reckless move.

The path behind her, she'd left in ruins, her quarters lurching from a precise blast before Sovereign or Karhl could follow her route. Slithering through ducts, gliding over regions that lacked gravity, the copious dress gathered up in her hands so legs might not tangle, she got close enough to feel the thud of Swelter's music.

Assuming there was a tracking device woven into her red silken prison, Quinn climbed faster, employing the most direct routes, guaranteeing she would arrive at her destination before Sovereign passed from the living quarters' decks.

She wanted them to see where she was heading, but she didn't want to give them time to catch her. More importantly, she wanted Drinta to grasp just who had put the ridiculous gown on her and why.

One vent stood between her and the Atrium; her entrance, the ground floor of the club. Drinta was at the center, twenty-three stories higher. Twenty-three stories of climbing walls with hardly a handhold, where old bullet holes served as the tiny crevices her fingers might cling to.

When the lights turned, flashing over another corner, Quinn slipped out, closing the vent to follow the shadows. Chin high, she walked as if she had a right to the final lift, over the last dais, interrupting conversations of those waiting to genuflect, shoving others out of her way. Two unknowns were thrown from the ramp to fall down into the club, guards having their weapons ripped from their grips so quickly they died before seeing just who had struck. The music, her speed, kept those in the inner sanctum unaware of her approach until she stepped onto Drinta's private balcony.

"Mistress Drinta." Quinn moved to the couch reserved for the few guests who were actually asked to sit. Someone of no importance to Quinn reclined in the seat she desired. He was thrown towards the exit, Quinn taking the vacant place and smoothing the infernal, dusty gown. "It is an honor."

The Tessan looked positively gleeful, entertained even as she motioned to her guards. "Are you valuable to me?"

"I am valuable to Sovereign, who has invaded your domain." Quinn didn't have time to fuck around. "He is on Pax with a contingent of Imperial soldiers, including Lord Commander Karhl."

The smile fell from green painted lips. "You must have a death wish to threaten me so."

Quinn growled. "You would do well to listen, bitch-queen. I'm a fan of the status quo and I find your leadership inspiring."

"You have ten seconds before I rip out your throat, human."

"Sovereign is on your station. He came here for me. I want off before I have to stomach his conversation for another moment. Open the byway, and I'll leave. He will follow. We each get what we want."

The Tessan threw back her head and laughed.

"Did you really think the Empire has come here to deal with you?" Quinn could sense she was edging the proper mental direction, seeing the changing in the tick of Drinta's emotion. "Did they conveniently offer you exorbitant gifts? So much that you began to grow suspicious? The tactic is an old one, designed to make you question yourself, to foster suspicion—to unbalance you. Their plan has been flawless. You shut down the byway and are trapped here. I am trapped here."

Drinta flicked her tail, motioning to her guards to hold position. "And just how would he take Pax?"

"I did not say take. Once he has me, Sovereign will destroy it." Lies flowed from Quinn's tongue like honey. "All it will cost him is one Herald, patience, and the artful application of riots. Should he get his way, you will have nowhere to run. In less than a cycle, I'll be in chains, and your head will be in a box."

Quinn could see Drinta contemplate the odds.

"In your case, it's the Tessan Authority he truly courts." Quinn sat like a queen and sneered. "And they are difficult to impress."

Drinta had not ruled for so long by being a fool. "You have no proof. Only pretty words."

Quinn reached for the glass left set aside by the last visitor, offering the last baited hook. "I feel him in my mind, you know, your imprisoned Kilactarin below. He will clarify."

The immediate deflation of amusement brought Drinta to narrow her eyes and look hard at what really sat before her. "Who are you?"

Swallowing the drink, keeping her face clear of emotion, Quinn answered. "I am Sigil, Imperial Consort of the Irdesian Empire."

Drinta's maniacal laugh welled up. "What an honor."

Quinn smiled, filthy gown and all. "The honor, bitch-queen, is all mine."

"And what is it that you want?"

"I want you to retain power over this pleasant slice of space." Her answer came hard. "If Sovereign takes me into custody, he will destroy Pax and you with it to further his aims. Or... you can open the byway. Where I go, Sovereign follows. I will draw him off. And knowing how much I adore this shithole, he'll leave it standing, dangling like a carrot, in hopes I find my way into whatever trap he has waiting should I return." Glancing towards the line of sycophants, Quinn found the Herald hastening towards the platform. "The next move is yours."

Quinn stood in unison with the Tessan, just as Arden cleared the gateway below.

He only looked to Quinn.

She glared back, smirking that he would not reach her in time.

The Tessan made no move to stop her retreat.

Fleeing through the levels, Quinn stripped, ripping at the red fabric until beads clattered upon the floor, until boning and wires, laces and grips, were all removed, and she was naked enough to disappear into the orgy.

Chapter 9

The Sudenovan she'd murdered for his armor *gifted* her uncleansed gear so foul, it turned Quinn's stomach. But it was worth the revulsion to stand near Drinta's balcony unseen, where no inch of pale flesh or plum hair was on display. Dressed as she was, she was only a mercenary gambling at *Torr*—and losing.

Hours had passed with no sound of the byway coming to life. Drinta still lounged on her platform with the Herald in attendance. There was no move on the Tessan's end to speak with the hidden Kilactarin slave below. The Empire was waiting her out. The Herald would stay in negotiation with Drinta long enough that Sovereign's mating would wear off. He would give the Tessan no time to explore what Quinn had told her.

The bitch-queen was not going to open the byway.

Options were severely limited. Without the slave collar, Quinn could not utilize many of the most useful access corridors. Not without drawing attention from overseers or setting off security programs. There were many species she could mimic, but she could not grow a Tessan tail, she could not *be* an overseer. That left maintenance shafts, air ducts, and public corridors at her disposal.

Hiding in plain sight was an advantage, but it also exasperated her weakness. She could feel them, the Empire, in Swelter with her. But as they could not see her, she could not see them. The constant itch of their presence was aggravating, paranoia making her nervous.

Creeping frustration made Quinn's hand shake, ruining her throw of the *Torr blaug* and earning the sneers of other patrons at the gambling table. After losing all the money she'd stolen, she stepped away.

She had to get to Que. Before that, she had to collect the sleeping child and steal a ship—so long as she could avoid falling into a bloodlust, that should be easy. But how the fuck was she going to get out without the goddamn byway online?

Why had Drinta not acted? What had that Herald said to her?

A pushy patron bumped her shoulder and Quinn threw a punch like a true Sudenovan. A brawl began, drawing all surrounding her into its vortex. It felt so good to rip through flesh, to break bone and work off her anger. But when a pile grew at her feet, when eyes turned to her, she realized her mistake.

She'd fought too well. She'd killed too many.

Already, scattered movement was coming her way. Imperials disguised as she was, slithering nearer to catch her. Sovereign must have suspected she'd lurk in the club, and in a foolish temper she'd given her position away.

Shouldering a blaster, Quinn shot randomly into the crowd, creating a panic that would offer cover so she might flee. Her solid armor may have reeked, but it also did well absorbing return fire. Out of dozens, only three shots made it through to pierce her torso, blow open her shoulder, and skim her forearm as she fled the riled mob.

If a hand grabbed her, she broke it. If rough arms circled her middle, smashing her to the ground, she became a tornado of violence. The brawl escalated, it sucked her in, it spat her out, and it claimed her blood until she'd crawled free to pant against a dark wall.

In that moment, all she wanted was the feel of Sovereign's throat in her hands, to watch the light drain out of his eyes. She could go to him—rip him apart before he knew she was in his shadow—and it would feel so good.

Bleeding where her fingers pressed her middle, Quinn stumbled off. She found a vent and fell all the way down to the base floor where she lay in misery—in such pain her mind stuttered. It was in that moment it dawned on her, the secret she needed to survive free.

Extreme physical damage muted her thoughts of rampage.

A bit of blood came from her mouth as she laughed.

Dealing with humans was usually so banal, but there was something about Arden that Drinta simply enjoyed. He was a charmer—a man who knew how to please—but she was not pleased with the smiling male now.

There was a subtle difference between rash decisions and immediate action. A creature of her years knew when to act and when to listen to lies with a smile. The byway would remain shut down for maintenance, Sovereign's presence or no. Control was important when dealing with power mongers, and the Empire needed to understand their place in her little corner of the universe.

They didn't have one.

"All this time, I thought you'd come to charm me. You're a sweet and pretty liar, Arden."

The Herald smiled, and shook his head as if innocent as a babe. "Don't let her lies distort what we share, pretty Drinta. Yes, we want her. But in all honesty, I didn't know she was here. Finding our delinquent skulking through your halls was an added... bonus to Pax's many pleasures. First and foremost though, you are my priority. That said, I think we both can grasp that she will need to be dealt with."

"And if I want to keep her?" Drinta settled back in her seat like a queen, cocked a brow, and waited for an answer.

It took some time for Arden to accede. "You like her."

Drinta blinked, her smirk neither growing nor diminishing. "She was a fascinating conversationalist. The title *bitch-queen* was spoken with such reverence. I think your human female admires me."

"Sigil is a psychopath, lacks empathy—is incapable of forming emotional attachments with her own species, let alone an alien one. It would be in your best interest to help us find her before she sets her contingency plan into motion."

"Contingency plan?"

"Consider how long the convict has hidden in your domain. She knows the ins and outs of Pax." Arden lounged comfortably, sedate. "You did not open the byway as she demanded. Her mental state leads to extreme reactions. She will try to force you. Were I in her position, I would systematically disable life support and cause the drivel collected in this mire to panic. She will have them do her dirty work for her."

No one forced Drinta, no one survived attempted manipulation, and liars she toyed with until she grew bored of the game. "Tell me, little soft-bellied Imperial, what did she do to warrant harvesting by a *Lord Commander*?"

As if admitting a minor wrongdoing, Arden grew serious and fractionally bowed his head. "That is classified."

Drinta flared her claws before her, inspecting each painted tip. "She titled herself Imperial Consort."

Smoothing a hand over golden hair, Arden laughed. "Sovereign may be a bit of a lecher—the man keeps hundreds of concubines all climbing over one another to earn his favor—but no, Sigil has never been one of them. She is a fugitive who has slaughtered many high-ranking Imperials. A dangerous fugitive who must be collected and returned to the Empire, where she will be made an example of."

Leaning nearer, tail flicking in warning, Drinta hissed, "Is Sovereign on my station?

The confusion on Arden's face, the way his brows drew nearer, was so well practiced, even Drinta was unsure if it was insincere.

The man shook his head, golden eyes sparkling as if the idea had grown droll. "Why would Sovereign leave the comforts of the capital to come to Pax?"

A definitive downward angle came to the reptile's brow; her voice grew terse. "So he is here."

Arden smiled, wicked as he licked his bottom lip. "You believe the tattling of a desperate woman? One who has not honored you as we have? I'm insulted, Drinta. You shake my faith in the glories of true arbitration."

He did know how to make her laugh. "Now you will tell me what it is your empire really wants. If I dislike the answer, I will feed you to my least favorite pet."

Adjusting the line of his tunic, the Herald sighed. "There is a feral human colony the Tessan Authority ignores, thus offering our enemies shelter. The byways in our power do not have access to that sector."

"Crossing the Authority so thoroughly would cause a war."

Arden shook a finger. "Never underestimate the art of tyranny and negotiation. The Authority will not risk outright war with our empire. Not over one planet of violent refugees."

The glint in her black eyes was anything but playful. "What if I were to take her side, Herald? What if I were to cease maintenance and open the byway?"

Games were over. "What do you want, pretty Drinta? What can the Empire offer you to keep that portal closed until she is in custody?"

"I enjoy seeing you shaken, which is good, as I have grown tired of your conversation." Arching her back, Drinta tapped a talon to her lips. "To be honest—and I rarely am—I believe the female."

Gone was the beautiful male, in his place was a creature that exuded menace. "Then you are already playing into her schemes. A pity."

"But I will help you catch her... on one condition." Gleeful, her glittering tail swished as she cooed. "I want to give Sovereign and his reluctant consort a gift, something only the *bitch-queen* of Pax could offer in continuing friendship between us. He shall accept it in person where all of Swelter might see."

Gunfire, more than the usual scattered burst, broke out a level below them, the shouts of the brawl loud enough to hear even through the force field separating Drinta's balcony from the madness.

"That would be Sigil—the terrorist you would invite to sit before you." Arden chuckled, stroking his chin. "I will admit I am eager to see just what she'll do."

Drinta did not spare the club a glance. She couldn't when it was far more important to watch the devious Herald's every move. "Do you know her well?"

The man smiled. How beautiful and how deadly he could look at once. "She is my sister, naughty thing that she is."

"And you gave her to Sovereign."

"When she was still a little girl, yes. It's customary to offer our emperor a noble family's prettiest daughters. But she ran away... and Sovereign is denied by no one. He wants her to prove a point. When she is returned, forced conversion will show our people that all can be united, that defectors will not be tolerated."

How cold the humans could be—it made Drinta all warm and fuzzy. "Interesting..."

"The sooner this *issue* is handled, the sooner you will receive just reward." Tapping his finger to his knee, Arden hesitated. "Out of curiosity, what are you going to demand in payment?"

"Nothing. All I really want is to watch you dance on my stage like every other whore in this pit." She waved him off, bored. "May our alliance continue, friendships persevere, and whatever other shit you nobles like to hear."

There was one way to put fear in the horrid creature preening before him. "I suggest you place a greater guard around you. Sigil will go straight for the throat."

Quinn woke hungry, her body having exhausted its stores repairing itself. Unsure how long she'd slept, she could only wonder if Sovereign had acted in her absence. It was difficult to tell, holed up as she was in a broken drainage line.

One thing was certain. The station did not shake. There was no persistent vibration of a functioning byway.

Groaning, pressing up from the ground, she held her hand to her belly and found she still bled sluggishly. Worse, her left shoulder had not fully reformed.

She needed nourishment for her body to mend.

The armor was gone, pieces of it torn off her in the battle, the remainder cast aside once she'd found the strength to flee the scene. Naked, she scuttled with the vermin, hissing when they took little bites where torn skin parted.

They'd probably been chewing on her the whole time she'd slept.

Smashing furry bodies with her fist, snapping at the sharp-toothed animals like a rabid dog, Sigil tore into their flesh and fed on foulness. There would be no survival if her arm didn't function. Crunching bones in her teeth, trying not to vomit, she consumed another scampering bastard.

Breath came easier, the susurrating noise of fleeing vermin faded, and drawing out a cry, her shoulder re-engaged, cartilage forming.

Blinking in the dark, filthy and alone, Quinn had to acknowledge that she'd survived worse. Much worse.

Condor...

And she hadn't been the only one. If her mother had eyes, Quinn was certain she would have looked upon her child's form with pity. But her mother had no eyes, just as her mother had no limbs—appendages had been removed, considered unnecessary for a living womb. Retrieving that torso had torn out Quinn's heart. Unplugging the mutilated Kilactarin from the machines that sustained her assured the only being who had ever loved her would die.

But Quinn didn't let that ruined creature expire on Condor. She took her mother away. She'd saved her, stolen the nearest shuttle, placed her mother in cryo where she did not have to suffer another day. Instead, her bearer died beside a river, neck painlessly broken by her child on a planet Quinn never knew the name of.

Death beside a river might be nice. Feeling the breeze, the sun... Que there beside her.

Sigil began to cry, scrubbing the tears and grime from her cheeks until sorrow turned to fury. Sovereign was responsible for all her miseries. She'd been made and tortured because of him. She'd been hounded, forced to live like a renegade simply because she'd been merciful and stupid in her youth.

There should never have been mercy. That had been her first mistake. On Pax she could kill him, slip right into his shadow and strike from the dark before he knew what monster slithered in his wake. Then Karhl, with his soft tone and placid expression—she could find ways to make him scream, to twist up that calm façade into torment.

They all had to die.

Excitement began, she cracked her neck, fantasizing about the pleasure of the hunt… then paused. Jamming her fingers in the closing hole beside her bellybutton, twisting them about her intestines, Quinn screamed. She couldn't heal yet—she had to stay wounded to stay sane.

She could not engage the enemy.

It was opening the byway that she had to focus on. Grab the cryotube, steal a ship, open the byway, find Que.

Chapter 10

Sovereign had called her perfect, but to think so was foolish. Nothing, no creature that had ever lived or would ever live, was flawless. Quinn's greatest defect was in the single-minded way she could behave. She wanted food, she took it. She found something pretty, it became hers. Life never mattered to her, only the false ideal of survival.

Que had taught her better, though it had not been easy for him.

After fleeing Condor, she and her mother had hibernated in cryo for years, their ship drifting aimlessly through space. The craft had been shot down, a panicked child waking in her shell to pound on a flight console she hardly understood.

Crashing in a foreign jungle had been painful. Parts of her ship had torn off on impact, left dangling in the trees. Alone, fire burning her skin black, she'd torn the cryotube holding her mother out of the hull and dragged it as far as she could.

But she was a little girl, grievously wounded, and could only get so far.

The cryotube was damaged and losing power. Soon it would fail, and the being within would be in agony.

There was a river, the child had never seen one before. Around it the earth was wet and squishy. Mud. She'd never felt it before.

When warning lights flashed, and the tube's power failed, Quinn opened the shell and looked down at her mommy. The Kilactarin was dying, in too much pain to sing properly for her daughter.

Quinn sang for her instead. She sang for the creature as she pulled her to the damp earth to feel mud. She sang for her mother as her hands went to her neck to know an embrace.

And she sang between sobs as the bones were snapped and the suffering creature's misery was ended.

There was no time to properly mourn. There was barely enough time to claw a grave into the earth by that river and cover up the body.

She sensed them coming nearer, the very scavengers who had shot down her ship had found her trail.

Human males. They found the child lying over a mound of fresh earth, weeping.

Her foot faced the wrong direction, an arm broken, in addition to the remaining damage had drawn no compassion from the bandits. They had put a leash on her as if she were a dog, dragging her through the mud as she refused to limp, refused to feel anything outside of grief for what she'd buried by the river.

What came next was nothing. Penetration had hurt. The laughter she had not liked. But so long as they tossed her scraps of food, she hardly noticed. How could she when her heart was broken?

It was three days before the worst damage mended. Three days that they played with their toy.

The sun was high in the sky when the last broken bone clicked into place.

A heavy body rutting her, the girl snapped out of her grief-stricken stupor. Without thought, Sigil ripped out her assailant's throat with her teeth. *She* laughed, as they had laughed at her when they'd taken their turns using up what they thought was a dying child.

When bodies began to pile up, and the little monster was seen feeding on the flesh, a few attempted escape on their ship. Flaring her psionics, she ripped the fleeing vessel from the clouds, pulling it closer as if she'd lassoed the moon. It crashed into the bandit's only shelter, both objects rendered useless.

Once they were trapped, once she tasted their fear, the order of her murder became an art. The bandits suffered in sequence of who touched her first.

She relished the fun, encouraging panic, screams, weeping… all the sounds they'd wanted her to make. As their numbers dwindled, Sigil tried to portion her food, picking them off over months.

Her last kill was a boy on the cusp of manhood, hardly old enough to warrant attention. But the teen had touched her, even if it was under pressure from his peers.

He'd tasted the *best*.

He was also the most terrified when the monster crawled from the jungle in the night, when she came for him when he was alone, weaponless, and stupid.

But then she was alone, with no human boy to taunt for weeks as she ate his petrified friends.

On Condor her greatest wish had been to be left alone. But true solitude on that unknown planet, it took from her. She ran wild, she screamed at storms, she challenged animals as large as mountains for sport. She cried... often.

Mostly she missed the way her mother used to whisper almost constant sweet music into her mind.

By the time Que discovered the emergency signal the bastards had set up in hopes someone might save them from her, Sigil had been reduced to a mindless nothing.

The Axirlan had shot the filthy beast on sight, no hesitation. Later she learned he'd carried her bullet ridden body onboard after seeing she was only a child—her filthy cheeks grimy and marked, by old and new tear stains. Even he knew wild children did not weep for no reason.

Sigil learned the word mercy.

There was food when she woke. He didn't try to touch her. The huge white being let her scramble about his ship, hiding where she would, for years. All that time Sigil never spoke, but as cycles passed, she did begin to watch.

In his dealings with others, he was steady. He allowed none who laid eyes on his pet to disrespect or mock her.

The creature just *was*.

Her first word to him was, "hungry," the Axirlan holding a sweet treat above her head where she could not reach it without either climbing him, which would require touching, or attacking to take it.

"Ask properly, child."

"GIVE!"

In response, Que ate the treat right in front of her. She'd cried as if the world was going to end, kicking her legs as she rolled on the floor.

"You must bathe, and you will wear clothes from now on." Another sweet was dropped to land on the screaming girl. "Food you take at the table, sitting while you eat. Most importantly"—knees bent, Que crouched over her—"you will not kill another guest who steps aboard this ship unless it is in self-defense. Do you understand, Quinn?"

Sigil ignored most things, she didn't care about where they were in the universe, but she always listened to that steady voice. But listening and *obeying* were two different things. Her cheeks stuffed full of the pastry, everything in her mouth so the alien could not take it, she scampered away.

It was another full month before he got her clean. A year before she would consider clothing. Words slowly appeared. Eventually she let him touch her. A pat was earned for good behavior, her ratted hair groomed if he could tempt her to sit still. In time, she could hardly bear to have him out of her sight, almost always leaving some part of her skin in contact with his mass, so that if he moved she'd know.

His sleeping mat became hers, Sigil—or Quinn as the man liked to call her— tucked against him to share warmth.

In all those difficult years he never hurt her. Never.

Even sex was something long forgotten until she saw the act between two Tessans.

They were visiting an outpost on a desert world to meet a supplier. At the table beside them, lovers played. Quinn could not look away, hardly understanding why the female seemed so involved, and felt... something... just by watching.

Over a decade she'd been with Que. Her body was no longer that of a child's, and she wanted to experience this strange thing. She climbed on the Axirlan there, hissing at the gaping supplier who sought to interrupt her explorations. Mimicking what the other female had done, she rolled her hips, she nipped and bit at her companion, and felt the organ between his legs grow hard.

"I want." Two words out of less than a hundred she'd spoken in a year.

Large hands grasped her hips, Que stilling her. "Tell me what you want, Quinn."

She hated when he tried to drag speech out of her. Gesturing impatiently, she said, "That."

"They are mating, Quinn. Joining their bodies for pleasure."

She rubbed against him, determined to get her way. "*I want.*"

The supplier was forgotten, Que initiating the first stages of sex. There, on a table in the middle of a second-rate bar, he showed her his member, a studded thing she had never seen erect. Eager, she scratched at him until he pulled aside the fabric over her mound and spread her wide in mimic of the Tessans.

The first thrust, the taste of Que's skin on her tongue, and an addict was born. All she wanted from that moment forward was to fuck him, to be fucked by him, to fight, to yield, to share. Others she found pretty were acquired, Que watching or joining.

Nothing was taboo.

Que encouraged it, as it was the first time he'd seen her play. The wild thing started to smile, but only for him. Full sentences, used mostly to describe things she wanted to feel, touch or do, demonstrated her healing was progressing. But the first disaster was not far off. With her sexual awakening came a gripping need that drove her to the point of madness. Not even a year later, she unexpectedly ran off after a stranger in a crowd only for Que to follow and find what his renegade pet had done.

The man, torn to pieces under her boots, was an Imperial Soldier far from home… as were the fifty other corpses on the docked ship she'd stolen. Shaking, pounding on the console in search of coordinates, Quinn growled. Que standing by, watching the girl raging at a machine she demanded take her to *Sovereign*.

When he approached, it was if she could not recognize him. When he spoke, she did not listen.

What he saw that day was a much stronger version of the monster he'd found scampering in a ruined settlement. He did what needed to be done. Que shot her until she was too damaged to move.

Then he placed her into cryo so he might assess what had gone wrong and attempt to fix it. The answer was in the misfiring of her brain, the agitated chemistry. He kept her under until Quinn normalized, and when he woke her years later, she clung to him.

She confessed what she was.

He took her as far from the Empire as he could.

Chapter 11

Sometimes when things went so wrong, it was good to know that they were actually going so very right. Lingering in the dark cell where her Kilactarin sat folded into a posture of meditation, Drinta cooed a sweet, "So, the human female sensed you. My little secret is out."

She took a step closer, looking over the wasted thing that had long since ceased to amuse her. "Before you speak, I want you to understand that the outcome of this chat will not change the fact that you are going to die. But... it will affect *how* you are going to die."

If that human woman had *any* talent for digging around in psychic brains, she might glimpse fragile intel Drinta would rather not share. One simple acknowledgment that the human *felt* Drinta's Kilactarin made the slave an absolute liability in the game the Mistress of Pax was very cunningly crafting.

The loose end would have to be ripped off... or neatly trimmed. That was up to the Kilactarin.

The cross-legged slave waved his long neck, moving to stand. "My death isn't the one you should seek. You must kill *her*, Mistress. Kill her at once."

It was the first time her prisoner had ever been forward, had ever offered a warning she had not painstakingly dug out of him. Smiling, she rubbed against her slave, her hand trailing over his torso. "Why?"

The Kilactarin, he was agitated. "*It* did not think like a human. She is unstable. Abnormal."

Drinta had a better word for it. "Valuable."

"No."

Sniffing at her prisoner, intrigued, Drinta purred, "What did you see in her mind?"

There was no immediate response, a thing highly unlike her mental spy.

Tickled all the way down to her toes, she witnessed her slave attempt to formulate deception. But his species lacked the skill, even if he'd heard her speak that beautiful language day in and day out.

The Kilactarin could not even form a lie, stuttering and choking on words.

Drinta flat out laughed. This was too good. "You fear that woman more than your own death?"

A different approach was attempted by the distraught alien. "The Herald lies. Sovereign is on the station. He came here for her. Nor was it anger or pride I sensed in the human male when he spoke of this Sigil. It was devotion. Obsession."

The backs of Drinta's lacquered talons ran the length of a thin Kilactarin arm. "I didn't ask you about Sovereign or the Herald. I asked you about the woman. Quickly now, tell me what you saw."

Wobbling its head back and forth, showing signs of actual panic, the Kilactrin confessed, "I saw evil. 'Psychopath' is not a strong enough description of what is wrong with her. Drinta, the abomination must *never* be allowed to leave this station. If you were to sense how damaged she is inside, what she might be capable of, you would grasp the danger."

Drinta smiled. She smiled and she considered.

"Damaged I can work with. Broken things like you are my specialty. Do you know your greatest flaw?" Her hand pressed over the lanky creature's lipless mouth when it parted to argue. "No, don't answer. I don't want to hear you speak again." A kiss was pressed where the Kilactarin's sensory node lay behind his skull. "You see so much, but understand *so* little. That pretty human would fit much better in your cage. And the best part is, I can see the cage will be unnecessary."

"If you can't kill that *thing*, abandon Pax to it. Destroy the byway so it can never get out of this quadrant. Let it starve to death!" Her Kilactarin was trying to argue, mumbled words struggling to work past the claw locked over his insufferable mouth.

"Enough." Eyes rolling, the Tessan silenced her slave's raving once and for all. Mercy had never been much fun, but she wasn't really in the mood for a bloodbath either. So, Drinta hooked one talon into the lean torso before her and ripped through flesh until the male's organs spilled out on the ground.

Smiling at her twitching work, the bitch-queen of Pax felt better than she had in days.

The slave had served her extraordinary information in those final moments.

What she could accomplish with the circumstances infecting her home would be nothing short of godly. When every little detail came together, the universe would know never to cross the *bitch-queen* of Pax.

Tears were only shed by the pathetic.

The warm rivulets on her cheeks, they were a byproduct of all the dirt she was dragging herself though. Her lip wasn't shaking, no, it was just a side effect of tension.

She was not afraid. That's not who Quinn was.

If she continued to deny, the terror, the pain, the sadness would not exist.

She told herself so, rebuking such weakness as she dragged her body through jagged metal debris and dust.

She was strong. The strongest. There was no one better.

Sovereign had tricked her, no more. He had tricked her, he had touched her, he had twisted her thoughts and threatened her friend.

But he didn't know her. He may have gathered intel, but he could never know just what lengths she was willing to go to.

Just as he'd never expect her to drag her body through Pax's garbage, feeding off detritus like a cockroach while simultaneously jabbing her fingers into the healing wound in her gut.

In order to stay sane, she had to maintain a cycle of recovery and damage, while ignoring constant pain and emergent apprehension. She couldn't waste a second giving in.

Time was more valuable than oxygen… which also happened to be thin within Pax's utility tubes.

She'd left a trail of blood in the refuse, red hand prints smeared here or there to delineate a path. Those little red stains were another reason she had to pull it together. Though the markers were few and far between, they were inevitably there.

Several alternating pathways had been used, circled back upon, misdirection the best she could offer the Empire. Sovereign or one of his Brothers would find that path. It was inevitable. Whether or not they fell for her trick, she did not know.

But she needed to keep them away from storage deck H7, bulk 673. The location of her sleeping Tessan boy, her Jerla, had to be prepared if her desperate plan was going to work.

The cryotube could not remain buried under rubble, not if she had only one slim chance to grab him. She would not have the luxury of appearing to syphon out trash. Once the byway was open, she'd steal a ship, ram the hull, and take him on board. Then she'd jam through the line at the byway, and get the fuck out of this corner of space.

Sovereign would pursue, but if she was clever, she'd get to Que first.

Her companion would take over from there.

Because they took care of each other. Always.

He would get her away from all of them. He would hide her someplace new.

It would only be his body that she felt beside her in bed. It would only be his hands, his pierced cock, and his strength.

No one else would be welcome to touch her.

Every time she thought of it, she saw red. Quinn could still taste his blood in her mouth, found herself inadvertently licking dry lips, and more than once realized she'd turned around and was crawling back toward her tormentor.

She had a battle of wills banding about her skull. Half of her wanted to hunt him down, whispered that should go to him, kill him, eat what was left. The other half, the sane half, was the one battling to control shaking hands and drag herself away.

It had taken hours longer to reach the sleeping child than she'd anticipated. An hour more to remove the layers of scrap she'd buried his cryotube under. But then there he was. She could have wept for the sight of him through the view window.

But she was already weeping.

Now all she had to do was drag the tonnage toward the loading dock, line it up for easy retrieval, and all would be well.

Panting, sweat burning her eyes, she took hold of it and yanked its mass step by step through piled scrap. It felt unnatural to struggle as she did, to be so weak. Every time the cryotube got caught in the junk, her heart would race all the faster. Every click of fallen debris and she was sure the Empire was coming for her.

Paranoia ate more at her belly than the gaping hole shot through it.

She bled a great deal, all over the tube, the garbage, the room. There would be no hiding it. But she could not think of that now, not when she was so close to having Jerla ready for transport.

Weak, and shaking from blood loss, Quinn fell inches from her goal, and found she could not get up. A jittery hand reached out for the nearest object, any kind of weapon, and enclosed upon a broken pipe.

That would do.

She needed rest, one short break.

Pipe in hand, she squeezed it tight, forced herself to keep her eyes open, and counted to one-thousand.

Break over, groaning from pain, she shimmied to her feet. Her eyes caught her sleeping child, and Quinn made a promise. "I promise you, boy, I will get you out of here. You won't wake up afraid like I did." Using her forearm to wipe grime from the view window, she looked down at his little face and whispered, "No bad men will drag you off."

"Her trail led into the subsections, through the water supply. We lost her on Division 5."

"It's not that you lost her, Karhl. It is that you failed by not searching every inch of her quarters for her escape hatch. You failed by not assuming her desperate scampering exit from Swelter would be so treacherous." Sovereign stood still, he spoke quietly, continuing the castigation he piled on the giant Lord Commander. "She has no care for her wellbeing. Pain is nothing to a creature who spent her youngest years tortured daily."

"Brother." The chimes in his hair sang as Karhl lowered his head in supplication. "Sigil knows the station. Giving chase might be what she wants. After your threat against the Axirlan, I fully believe she would kill you if given the chance, impulse or no. Her feelings on the matter will not change."

Sovereign looked over the rumpled bed. "She is afraid of me."

"Very." Karhl agreed. "But she is more afraid of what you might do to her companion."

Arms folded behind his back, Sovereign measured the large warrior. "Her fear for you is less acute."

"Had you seen how she smirked at Arden's approach in Swelter... *He,* she does not fear at all." Glacial eyes followed the movement of his leader. "Invite her to sit with him. Let him woo her. You are too tempting to her indoctrination and I lack the skill to inspire her love."

Pausing, Sovereign disagreed. "Arden lacks the strength to subdue her. His chance of survival should she attack is miniscule. Aside from the loss of a dear Brother, should she kill him, she would regret it later. Such an action would cause her pain."

"Whatever she is doing to fight the impulse puts her at risk. Her wounds from the fight, even the fall, would have caused great damage. She may be weak." Karhl looked at his Brother, his leader, his superior. "She may not run from the Herald as she would from us."

A brief ripple of emotion passed over the emperor's stone-cold eyes. "In order to have avoided the impulse for such a time, she must be utilizing pain. I can practically hear the muffled screams. Sigil thinks to wait for the byway to open, where she will stumble to it, bleeding and drained."

"Then we open the byway and draw her out."

"No!" The answer came sharp, the room even shook from a momentary lapse in cold control. "Sigil has the ability and training to get what she wants. I believe she will push herself to the point of suicide. She won't go back to Swelter or think to sway Drinta again, but she will try to force Pax's mistress to act." Sovereign warned the Lord Commander, "In her desperation, she will place herself at great risk. There is no room for failure again. I expect better from you."

The castigation was accepted fully. "What are my orders?"

"Find her." The emperor grew dark, and a minute amount of his great anger was allowed to show. "When Sigil is found we shall follow your suggestion. Only Arden may approach. He will seduce, and you will tighten the net around her."

Chapter 12

Absolutely filthy, Quinn's fist rapped hard enough on the door to leave a dint. It wasn't like one more flaw in the metal would be noticed… nor would the smear of bloody dirt. Nothing in Pax was pristine.

The glorious station was as disgusting as the grime-smeared woman seeking shelter.

Aggravated sounds came from the other side of that portal. She banged again until the hiss of hydraulics signaled that the unlucky occupants had chosen to answer.

There were three of them. After Quinn took four steps into their abode, two remained.

By the time the door had fully closed behind her, there was one.

Until there were none.

They never stood a chance against the stinking intruder with her pipe and snapping teeth. Quinn didn't know who they were, and it didn't matter. Good people didn't lurk on Pax.

There wasn't time for extra emotions like remorse.

Part one of her plan had been set into motion. Jerla had been secured for imminent retrieval. But Quinn could not make a move to grab him until she'd stolen a ship. Doing so would be pointless until the byway was opened. Otherwise, there was a chance others would notice and Sovereign would have her cornered. Haunting Pax gave her many places to hide. A foreign ship with unknown corridors and occupants, did not.

The domicile she'd appropriated was clean, barring the previous occupants' corpses haphazardly piled in the corner. There were dried foodstuffs, a bathing cubicle, and plenty of Bailor clothing.

Quinn needed a shower, she was desperate for real food, but before she could indulge her wound riddled body, she needed to find some self-control.

Every minute, she slipped a little bit more, obsessed deeper, and hungered for the hunt.

She had to do something to stop herself, and she had to do it at once.

Back to the wall, Quinn looked at the broken pipe in her hand, knowing what she had to do. Considering all that had been endured in her lifetime, she found it almost funny how she hesitated. Three deep breaths, a long swig of stolen *wevd* liquor, and she lined up the jagged tip with her abdominal wound. One quick thrust and she stabbed it in until everything she'd just swallowed came back up.

The remainder of the *wevd* was sucked down, intoxication preferable to outright misery. Quinn knew what the sheep expected. The most plausible next step would be to systematically destroy critical life support so the armed menagerie on Pax might overthrow their mistress and reopen the byway in a panic.

She wasn't that stupid.

Drinta had sided with the Empire. The whole station was against Quinn now. Security checks required the removal of helmets at all key access points. Scans for human female bodies were randomly executed down corridors and in domiciles.

Places Sovereign or Drinta counted as vulnerable would be surrounded by an army.

Good thing Quinn had a better idea of what the term *vulnerable* meant.

Escape would require creative pressure, small actions that would set the station scrambling without drawing attention her way. She understood the patchwork wiring and maintenance of the station in a way no engineer slave in Drinta's service knew it. There were weaknesses in the circulatory system of electricity, of the water pooling in forgotten cisterns on abandoned decks.

She would poison with apprehension, certain Drinta's collected mercenaries were already aware of tightened security but ignorant of the reason. She would scare them, let them create their own fictions as to what was going on within Pax—let the rumors become a beast.

Eyes sticky, upper and lower lashes gumming together with each blink. Quinn rubbed the crust away, each movement of her arm fostering sharp pain in her oozing abdomen.

Water—she needed water.

Parched, Quinn stumbled to the sink and found she could not bend down to drink straight from the spout. Panting, looking around the room, she found a cup, filled it, and drank.

Swallowing past her sore throat felt like bliss, but keeping that water down once it hit her gut was a battle.

A building fever set her head to aching, the open flesh around the pipe growing red and puffed—horrid looking. But impaled, there were no mindless thoughts of stalking Sovereign.

She should have stabbed herself hours ago.

Standing in the bathing cubicle under the cooling chemical spray, all the grime and blood ran down the drain. Clothing was acquired from what lay scattered in the room. The smaller species' padded jacket much easier to move in than Sudenovan plate mail, now that she was skewered by a metal rod.

The black even did a decent job of concealing accumulating blood and pus that leaked out her middle.

Grabbing fistfuls of plum-stained hair, between fits of coughing, she carelessly hacked it off. When left with nothing but mismatching tufts, the edge of a nearby knife was dragged over her scalp. By the time it was finished, she was covered in sweat, and desperate for more water.

Water would have to wait.

Bald as an egg, she braced her hands to the wall, took a deep breath, and slammed her face against it. With a muffled crack and a pink mist of bloody spittle, her nose broke, flattened and twisted to the side. Blood came thick, caught with a stolen length of cloth, while she mushed it down further.

No reflection was required for Quinn to know her appearance had altered significantly. The flattened nose and subsequent swelling masked the dancer from Swelter, and offered instead the ugly face of any patron who might go there to fuck.

She dropped the blood soaked rag and smiled through the gore.

There was more work to do to see her though the plague Quinn intended to bring upon the inhabitants of Pax.

Every last potential container in the room had to be filled with water and stored for future use. The apartment had to be searched for anything she might deem useful.

Cutting a glance to the pile of corpses in the corner, Quinn started her search there. Money, weapons, anything of use was taken. But no matter how she cursed or how roughly she tore at pockets, no ship token of any kind was found.

These were crew, not captain.

Which meant they might be missed.

Well, if anyone came knocking, more corpses would be piled up in the corner.

When all possible vessels were filled to the brim with Pax's murky water, Quinn limped into the halls.

Little attention was paid the lurching passerby.

Blood loss was slow but continuous, leaving Quinn breathless as she found her way. She made it past three checkpoints and two overseers' stations to find the blockaded corridor that would solve all her problems.

Subsection B-46 no longer hosted life on the station. A radiation leak long before Quinn's arrival had made the area unsuitable. It was forgotten, so dangerous that even Quinn had never entered.

Until now.

In that region water sat stagnant, irradiated, and cut off from the main supply. But there were *drainage* pipelines—small ones that had not been demolished—where shored up valves held a trickle of poison. As the station's segments were identical in design, if Quinn was fast, she could race through crumbling tunnels and redirect the clogged drainage. There would be no immediately noticeable change, but eventually ruined water would run through inadequate filters, until recirculated into the main supply for consumption, poisoned with radiation Pax's purification system could never remove.

Drinta's little army would grow ill. Swelter would grow vacant. Gangs would seek their ships for clean water... plagued with boredom and disease as they sat hanging on the dried up tit of a black hole—because, just like her, they would not be able to leave until the byway was open.

Idle mercenaries did interesting things, finger pointing being one of the best.

It wasn't difficult to shift the rusted access panel, no security was there to stop her, and in mere minutes she was racing through the tomb-like segment of hell.

Right where it should have been sat a silent valve.

Laughing under ragged breath, Quinn put her weight against the first rusted wheel and turned until metal groaned. The sound of the pressure, of the flow once released, was unmistakable. She ran to another, finding it would not turn, and abandoned it for the last valve before radiation caused more harm than even her body could mend.

Like its predecessor, the value would not turn. She fought the damn thing, cursing until she began to see double.

Head pounding, gut turning to mush, she went to her knees and swallowed back bile.

From the corner of her eyes she saw a flash of black and gold.

Fever, exposure, infection... that had to account for why she would have sworn the pretty one, the golden emissary was standing in the shadows watching her.

Stolen blaster in her blistered hand, she shot right at the phantom, only to blink and see nothing but fresh holes in a grimy wall.

There was nothing there, no blood, no Imperial psyche pushing her beyond the pale.

Her mind was playing tricks on her, and cowing to hallucinations was going to get her killed

A shaking hand holstered her weapon, Quinn fighting to stand so she might finish her work.

Straining, she found the wheel would not turn no matter how she attacked it or how hard she pushed. Screaming obscenities into the dark, blinking only to find the phantom Imperial watched from another, nearer corner, her footing slipped and the wheel won.

One leaking pipe of poison would not be enough. The contamination would take too long.

Her plan was failing before her eyes.

Looking to where the blurry Herald waited, she pulled herself up and let out a snort. Once again, it had come closer, stood directly across from her, bracing the very lever she'd been unable to turn.

The pipes gave a shutter as the wheel loosened. It gave, water flowed, and Quinn ran.

Dodging debris, leather sticking grossly to her sweaty body, she made it out, sealing the exit so no nightmares could follow.

No Imperial followed her trail. All of it had been her fear working on her.

There had never been anyone there.

Chapter 13

The lights flickered again, disruption of the electric system ushering rolling brownouts through key sectors.

"Sigil." Sovereign said the name with pride. Looking to the unsmiling Lord Commander Karhl, he added, "How clever she is."

They could feel her in the room each time the lights dimmed. It made her real to the men who had spent a century searching every corner of space for their woman.

She was so close they could taste her in the air. And if it meant crushing the station to draw her into their embrace, Sovereign and his Brothers would do so with a smile.

There was no limit to what they were willing to do.

None.

It was only a matter of time before they would have her.

All four of Karhl's warriors stood at data panels, breaking down information at inhuman speed, all in an effort to pinpoint their prey's latest disturbance. The hybrids had no answers, the grid sparking in too many places to signal where the heart of the infection lay, or what the point of it might be. Her latest attack did nothing to truly upset the system.

She was taunting them.

Side by side, two powerful creatures capable of very dark things looked on and saw what the quasi-humans missed—her game with the power was only a message. It wasn't in words; it was in deeds.

She'd held out five full cycles, brought havoc to Pax. In that time, the water had been deemed undrinkable. A great many had been poisoned from something as innocent as an ice cube, making potassium iodide the hottest rare commodity on Pax's trading floors. But there had been a flaw. It would seem Sigil's trick had only polluted the free sectors. Slaves' poor quality water was separate and unaffected.

Though many of Drinta's guests had left to seek solace on their ships, the less scrupulous hadn't. Instead, they pushed the most vulnerable aside, unconcerned with the suffering of the slaves to commandeer their drinking water.

"She will grow angry her ploy failed," Karhl had said when slave quarters were overrun, a great deal of young and old thrown out into the vacuum of space. "Our female will act out. She will expose herself."

But she had not, and that in itself was telling. She was unaware of the overall state of Pax. Her guerrilla attacks were pinpoint, precise—moves based off assumption, almost childlike. Through it, Sigil was hidden away outside of her revenges with no real notion of the spectacle that played out on her Pax. And it was *her* Pax; Drinta was only a custodian, though the Tessan female did not quite understand her place.

Sovereign looked around the Imperial command station set up in Sigil's quarters, eyes roving over rusted walls and the bowing ceiling, and saw her in the shade of her linens, in the scent of her discarded clothing.

In his pocket was the very strip of leather he'd ripped from between her legs before he'd liberated her mind from madness. It smelled more beautiful than the rarest wine.

He'd not had the luxury of tasting her there yet, but the man knew, one lick and he'd be an addict. Sovereign could imagine nothing more perfect than his female on her back, her legs spread wide open for his mouth, hour after hour of her cries filling the air.

She would be spoiled with caresses and sweet words, with violence and the pain she enjoyed.

He would share her, but Sigil would always be his. His Imperial consort.

This fear she harbored, she would be broken of it. How little she understood her pursuers, or why they chased. How little she understood herself.

Karhl had tried to explain, he had tried to be gentle, careful. Sigil wasn't capable of listening; not yet. But it had given her perspective to consider. With their help, her natural impulses could be curbed, untwisted from Commander Demetri's conditioning and reformed to intermesh perfectly with their needs.

They could, they *would*, help her.

By any means necessary.

Sovereign knew exactly what she'd lived through. He had forced himself to watch every last recording found in Condor's archives. Even knowing the extent of Dimitri's depravity, they all had assumed she'd lived the same austere training and upbringing they had. Never could they have anticipated what was going on during those years.

Sovereign had watched the little girl's suffering; he had memorized the sound of her fear. On the view screen, a monster had been born.

A horribly abused child grew capable of carnage. The things Dimitri had had her do…

A black hole and something far more horrific than guilt were left where his heart should have been. Her screams had been Sovereign's anthem, the music of his enemies' cries never loud enough to drown hers out.

"Arden has failed to establish contact for two cycles. He purposely evades my seekers. The little bastard even disabled his communicator." It wasn't Pax's flaring circuitry that held Karhl's concentration, it was the strategy he'd enacted and the lack of response from the Herald sent on the mission.

Amongst their Brothers, alive and dead, there had never been a greater infiltrator than Arden. None was more cunning.

Sovereign should know. He'd raised and trained the man.

Unconcerned, the emperor gave a flat response. "If she had killed him, Sigil would string up the corpse for us to find."

Karhl was not contented, not after so many cycles with no signs of Sigil except her pranks. "Disobeying outright orders—disconnecting—endangers her. I want her back here. I want her safe."

Eyes full of violence turned to the Lord Commander. Sovereign's calculating demeanor slipped and rage marred sculpted beauty. "You would dare question my intent? No one wants that more than I! Arden is doing exactly what he was ordered to do. He is building rapport with our antisocial runaway. His silence we must bear. To alter the plan now would reset the playing board."

"Brother—"

The snap of his words, the perfect articulation… Sovereign buried the rage, the jealousy, and the hostility, while simultaneously threatening a soldier of great power. "You requested this path, and now you complain. Was it not you who wished to rear her gently, to not terrorize her back into our care?"

The Lord Commander demanded an explanation for his leader's acceptance of insubordination. "Excluding us assists how?"

Unlike the Lord Commander, Sovereign understood exactly why they were kept waiting. "He knows we lack the restraint to stay away if we knew where she was. What he does, he feels is best for the ultimate outcome."

"Pax already trembles from the weight of too many inhabitants, the lack of sufficient resources, and no water. It is only a matter of time before the entire system fails, unless Drinta opens the byway and relieves the burden." The Lord Commander changed tactics. "What if Sigil has captured Arden? What if his death was days ago and she seeks dramatics in the display of her kill?" Karhl stepped nearer, meeting the terrible eyes of his strongest Brother. "What if she uses his body to mute her conditioning?"

That was a possibility Sovereign had already considered. Such thoughts had filled him with wretched covetousness that ate away at his guts. "His timeline does not expire until the end of this cycle. Arden has seven more hours until I order a full-scale occupation. If he's failed, once Pax is ours, we'll rip the decks off piece by piece until we find her."

Successfully tainting the water supply had required extensive decontamination of her body. After it was done, Quinn had run the shower, chemical spray rinsing over her for over an hour. Her clothing had been left in a garbage chute, her skin scrubbed over and over—even eyes, ears, nose, and mouth. After two days, there were hardly any burns to show for her time in the irradiated corridors. The only side-effects she'd come away with, a dry cough and the same steady fever. But at least there had been no more hallucinations—only the one that refused to leave.

She was certain the Herald wasn't there. She'd shot at him enough times her blaster was out of plasma, gaining nothing more than a smattering of holes in the walls.

Madness was something she'd lived with her whole life. Madness was familiar. The easy solution was to ignore the pretty phantom.

But it began to speak to her.

Golden eyes glanced down to where the pipe protruded from her torso. "You are in pain."

Quinn disregarded the apprehensive imagining, working to steady her shaking hand so she might twist more wires together over the circuit boards she'd pilfered. There were five more to go, five more hours of tedious distraction.

Each time a wave of nausea hit, she dug her nails into her palms in an effort to keep her momentum moving forward. Between constant vomiting and the throbbing inside her skull, it was almost easy to ignore how Pax's air was practically saturated in the smell of Sovereign.

Sovereign.

She made a noise in her throat, a starved groan when thoughts slipped and she wondered if his flesh would taste as good, as delicious, as his blood. It was almost a reflex now, how her hands would reach for and twist the pipe to the point she almost blacked out.

She was holding out beautifully. Sovereign was never going to have her. Quinn would disembowel herself first.

Warm breath ghosted over her ear. "Don't do that."

Wheezing, using the table for support, she threw one of her circuit boards at the image. "Be quiet, devil. I'll do anything it takes to get to Que!"

"You wouldn't do *anything*..." The Herald gave her a playful look, standing incongruously beside her water supply, his fingers dancing over the liquid. "You would not submit to Sovereign for Que."

Chuckling hurt. In fact, it brought pure agony to her wrecked body, and ended in dry, wheezing coughs.

When she caught her breath, it was almost easy to ignore the hovering ghost.

A few more hours of dedicated focus and the circuitry was finished. Ignoring the lurking phantom trailing her through the room, Quinn ate what she could find in the cupboards, drank as much water as she could hold before the need to vomit warned she'd better stop, then left her newly acquired rooms to install damaged regulators randomly throughout the station.

Trying to find them kept Drinta's goons busy, thinned out the guards at each checkpoint, and was simply amusing to the woman poking the beast with a stick.

Most importantly, the continuous disruptions upset those who lingered onboard.

But it was exhausting work. By the time she was finished installing the last bit of circuitry, Quinn lost her footing and fell back against a crumbling corridor's wall. Crumbled, bleeding, whispering fevered nonsense, she almost faded out of consciousness. Lights began to flicker. Lips twitching, she laughed at such a silly victory.

Victory deserved reward. A moment's rest. After all, she'd earned it.

Head lolling back, sweat dripped through the stubbled new growth on her skull and down the back of her neck. All that heat radiating off of her, yet she was freezing.

So cold.

So tired.

Blurred vision gave the walls the distinct impression that they were melting, closing in around her. She was to be buried by them, covered to sleep forever in the place she loved most.

Lids dragged over swollen eyes, exhaustion dragging her into perilous slumber right there out in the open.

She couldn't even remember why she was supposed to get up. Whatever it was no longer mattered.

All that mattered was sleep.

She dreamed of the smell of heaven, of cool water down a parched throat, of painless breaths that enriched her.

Muttering to the air, she spoke to Que, assuring him she was coming for him. In answer, he brushed a cool cloth over her forehead. "Tell me of Sovereign."

She was lying upon a bed, unsure how she got there. "I hate him."

"Why?"

Vertigo overtook her, as did the shadow of anger, and the far greater demon of fear. "He *bit* me and I couldn't move. Sovereign fucked me and *made* me like it."

Fingers smoothed over the fuzz on her scalp. "You felt forced. You were frightened. It was a terrible thing."

It wasn't Que cradling her when the vertigo passed. Blurry vision showed she had only her phantom for company. "You're not real."

The Herald held a cup to her cracked lips. Quinn refused it, turning her face away.

The dark grew silent. She found the ghost gone, and agony-drugged sleep returned. She burned amidst great shivers, full of anger and fear, and the constant voice of a phantom she wished would shut up. Rage came so strong it filled her to the point her skin was too small, too tight to contain it.

There was a delicious smell in the air.

Sovereign.

Sovereign was so close—so ripe for the killing.

She woke, slick with sweat, a sharp weapon already in her grip. Snarling, squeezing the filth smattered pipe, Quinn held it up to inspect the lovely shiv. That gross matter already clung to it, that it was rusted and jagged, would only cause Sovereign more pain when she drove it into him *over* and *over*.

Unfortunately, the hallucination of the Herald was gone.

Too bad...

It would have been fun to spear him first, wear his beauty like a coat when she stalked and confronted his Brother.

Morbid ideas collected, piling up atop one another before she could process which direction, which style of murder, would be best. Thank the gods she'd slept, that her burns and abdominal wounds had knit together. Debilitating pain had curbed far too much of her fun—interfered with what should have been a delicious hunt.

Rolling to her hip, her brain sloshed against her skull.

Licking cracked lips, Quinn stumbled right past the stored water her body required. The exit was only a few paces away, but a toe caught on something unseen. Tumbling forward, her forehead smacked the ground.

Blinking, looking again at the black caked pipe in her hand, waiting for her vision to sharpen... she grew confused.

Why was she holding the pipe?

That's not where it was supposed to be.

Flopping to her back, she shucked her spare hand up the line of metal, flinging the black, sticky remnants of her guts on the floor. Her belly was swollen, protruding and tender... but her wound was closed. Soon it would be healed.

Holding on to the fragile moment of clarity, Quinn put her wrist between her teeth. Screams were easy, but screams were for the weak and would draw attention. Instead she bit down on her wrist until it bled, until her mouth pooled with the taste of copper and captured groans, and drove the pipe right back into her belly.

"Why are you doing this?"

Immobile from unimaginable pain, dazed, she stared at the return of her lingering phantom. A clumsy mouth said, "I told you. I have to get to Que. He'll worry."

The hallucination's voice was the same temperate tone in every conversation they'd shared. "Axirlans are incapable of feeling worry."

"Shut up."

Arguing with it was pointless. Shuffling on hands and knees, Quinn ignored the insolent apparition in favor of her buckets for a drink.

Draped in black, it crept closer, the golden embroidery displaying an Imperial tunic of high rank. "If he means so much to you, so much that you would mutilate yourself, why not demand Sovereign let you keep him? Is that not a better idea than failed sabotage and dangerous self-harm?"

Stumped, swallowing down greedy gulps of untainted water, Quinn coughed out, "Sovereign would kill him. He would lock me in a room and breed me until I died. I won't fall for your lies."

"He needs you. You know that." The voice modulated like a caress, perfectly comforting and reasonable. "Think of your power. Your Brothers desire that you be willing, happy. Concessions could be made. Go to Sovereign and demand what you want. Let him love you."

She closed her eyes, resting her aching head against the lip of a full bucket, and began to doze.

The Herald's voice tickled her ear, "Imagine your Que watching you raise your children... a guardian steadfast and loyal, as you say. There need be no struggle, no pain. *You could keep him.*"

Cooling touch stroked like a feather over her stubbled skull. It felt so good, she lolled, Quinn clinging to the container before sagging to the floor.

Pure reason, sweet tones, and more gentle touches came with the words, "If you continue as you are, you'll never make it. If I had not been watching, you would have succumbed to fever days ago. You can hardly stand. Even if the old hag were to open the byway, how will you commandeer a ship? How will you fly it? Embrace that at *this* moment you are the frontrunner in this little game, but if Sovereign catches you..." The soothing whisper stopped, a tongue tutting for a moment. "*When* he catches you, there will be no parlay."

Pressure came to her temples, fingers rubbing circles where her head ached. Wilting, she found something waiting to pillow her shoulder and neck.

Delirious, she looked up at the Imperial and pleaded. "Don't... take the pipe out... again."

"Shhhhhhhh, Sweet Sigil. I know what's best. Relax and listen to my offer."

She squirmed as if she meant to rise, and fell back, pain muted by the intoxicating coolness of more water brought to her lips.

"Imagine the pleasures, little firebrand. Imagine the joys." He adjusted her neck to a more comfortable angle. Tear stains were wiped away with the hem of an embroidered sleeve. "A life where you will always feel safe."

A deep phlegmy breath, her torso complaining at the pressure inhalation put on the swelling, and Quinn found herself unable to answer with more than, "Lies..."

"He *will* learn how to best behave with you once given the chance. Every single one of your Brothers will adapt. So long as you retain discomfort in the presence of humans, only family will be allowed near you. If you feel overcrowded, then sanctuary will be offered, alone or in the arms of whomever you deem fitting. Have I not shown you how careful we can be?"

Looking up into the golden eyes of the man whose black clad thigh pillowed her head, Quinn felt more stinging liquid slip from the corner of her eyes. "I don't feel safe. I don't... feel well."

"I know." There was nothing but compassion in the response. "Your pipe is made of lead. You've exposed yourself to the point of infection. The overdose has caused a decline in mental functioning, blurred vision, and a raging fever."

A laugh cut through her blubbering, the sense of relief drawing a smile. "That's right... you're not real. Only a hallucination brought on by blood loss, indoctrination, and lead poisoning."

Fingers went back to circling her temples, the man nodding. "I am very real, Sigil. Every time we've spoken it's been real. You told me about your mother, about how much you dislike dry places... how you hated Sovereign's bite."

Unable to stop chuckling, licking at the blood crusted at the corner of her mouth, Quinn argued, "If you were real you would not have helped me sabotage the water supply."

"You are quite the troublemaker. So vindictive when you do not get your way." A deep snort, an amused chuckle, preceded, "It was fun."

Sagging further to the scuffed floor, Quinn sighed, "If you take out the pipe... you know I'll kill you."

The apparition shrugged as if it were nothing. "I'm much faster than you, Sigil. You've missed with every shot." His fist closed over the stump angled outside her belly, yanking the weapon out. As she convulsed, he threw it far out of her reach.

The faint sound of the lead pipe hitting the floor registered, but not so much as fresh liquid warmth seeping from her belly to track down her sides. Eyes squeezed shut from pain, she growled, "Don't call me Sigil!"

A brush of a fingertip followed the shape of her lips. "I will call you Quinn if it would make you smile for me again."

"There is no Quinn without Que."

A kiss touched a burning forehead. "I envy your Que."

She could not help but agree. "So do I. He's on the right side of the byway and far away from you."

"Now, that was not very nice, my darling." Again his sleeve wiped at tears and the beading sweat. "There is not much time until you heal to the point madness replaces illness. What is to be your fate? Will you go to him? Will you make your demands and return to us on your terms? Or do we wait until he finds you?"

Her eyes were already closing, the feeling of more blood seeping, leaving her boneless. "I... want to sleep."

"No. Eyes open!" He jarred her just enough to earn a flared look of pained hatred. "You cannot sleep now. Now is the time you tell me what you want."

She began to cry from exhaustion. "I just want to go home."

Her ghost looked a little sad. "Where is home?"

"Que. Que is my home."

Hands lifted her from the floor, arms beneath her generating the sensation of floating until her feet were placed on the ground and she was forced to stand. The Herald slung her arm high around his shoulders, helped her press a hand to where her abdomen oozed.

"Come, my dear Quinn. We shall walk to Sovereign. The journey will clear your head."

She could hardly manage her steps, would never have made it had the Herald not borne the majority of her weight.

The man was right, the farther they moved, more clarity came. Once her ploy with Drinta failed, there had never been a chance to leave Pax. Too many days had passed, each hour twisting her mind all the more. The damage it took to keep herself under control was too extensive. There would never have been a plan she could carry forth, damaged as she was.

She'd failed.

Turning to look at the profile of the Herald, studying the clean line of his jaw and how his long, braided hair had grown messy from the time he'd spent in her presence, she choked out the question, "Why are you doing this? Why didn't you just drop me at Sovereign's feet?"

The smile, the sincerity of his offer velvet, Arden promised, "Because I'm on your side."

"If he won't give me Que"—she only had one threat left—"I'll rip out my throat. There will be no dynasty."

"The thought of such a thing, of this hate you bear for yourself"— too much sadness moved through golden eyes—"it gives me pain."

Quinn held his gaze. She stared through any softness to the core of the monster in his pretty shell. "You do not know what *pain* is, Herald."

"My name is Arden. And I do not know pain as you have known pain," he agreed, continuing their mission forward no matter how often her feet dragged. Careful of her smaller stature, of her labored breath he said, "But I do know longing. I do know that our family has suffered with their loneliness for you. And I know that you ache for them, even though you do not know the why of it. That is why you must hold on to me. I'm going to see you through."

Quinn forced her dangling legs to take another step for Que. "You're going to take me home."

"Yes."

Chapter 14

The Herald had fulfilled his mission with hardly an hour to spare.

Arden succeeded in his duty, brought Sigil willingly back to them, but her stolen clothing had been clotted with blood, her face a landscape of swelling and bruises. There were no plum stained waves, but a bare skull fuzzed with new growth.

Far worse than how she'd appeared was the reek of decay oozing from the broken thing's very breath.

Once she'd stumbled through the door with only Arden's strength keeping her on her feet, the female had gripped her throat with one hand, nails digging in to the point a little river of red ran freely down dirty skin. In a voice as desperate as her actions, she'd hissed, "Stay back and we will speak. Come nearer and you will not like what I'll do."

"How did this happen?" Karhl, huge, armored in the weighty black matte of Imperial military, stared at her blood-crusted torso, furious with the Herald who dared return her in such a state.

When the Lord Commander continued to approach her, Sovereign caught his arm and held Karhl still, unwilling to view more red flow from his female's neck.

"Our little vagrant stabbed herself with a lead pipe," Arden gently explained, winking at the furious monster he'd retrieved. "She was skewered with it the whole time she terrorized Pax."

"Sigil..." The white-haired warrior looked on as if the statement gave him pain, as if he too had borne days of suffering impaled by a rusted cylinder.

It was the first expression Quinn had seen on Karhl's face, and every person gathered in that room could see she didn't understand why it would be there.

She looked baffled, even slightly disgusted by his concern.

Her eyes left the overlarge Karhl and settled upon the greater threat.

Sovereign knew the assassin inside her sized him up. That she found him more dangerous, even with his relaxed stance and leaner build, than the bulky Lord Commander at his side.

She'd yet to come to terms with the fact he'd defeated her once.

No... they both knew he'd defeated her *twice*.

The state she'd arrived in was... dangerous. The things she'd done to herself, horrendous. But it was the claw buried millimeters from her carotid artery that forced Sovereign to concede. In a voice soft and generous, he asked her to speak. "What do you desire, precious Sigil?"

"Que." So much fear lay on one battered expression; so much fatigue. The way the skin crinkled at the edges of her eyes, betrayed her. His Sigil knew she could not fight him, knew she couldn't win. With things as they were, the only thing she could do was make a last ditch effort or die. "I will keep my friend, forever. And you will keep us safe."

Sovereign's answer was breathless, "You seek to force *me*?"

She did. Choking on the words, she made her offer, "And if you do this, I will submit to you."

Dark hair swung forward past his jaw when he lowered his chin. It cast a shadow, made him look all the more beautiful and sinister. "I want you to *love me*, to love us all."

"I WOULD NEVER LOVE YOU IF YOU TOOK ME FROM QUE!" Her shriek cost Sigil a great deal of effort, both Karhl and Sovereign tensing to control themselves to see her doubled over in pain. Panting, bracing against her grip on Arden, she looked from under her brows and swore. "You think you know the mind of their kind? You think he would abandon me? You have been too long with humans to understand. And I would *never* abandon him either!"

Karhl cocked his head, calling her attention with the chimes in his hair. "Young one, please calm yourself. You are too damaged for such displays."

"Fuck you." The woman drew more blood to spill down her neck. "I want an answer."

Arden, attempting to pacify his cargo with a careful stroke, smiled as if all were well. "Let's not exasperate her, shall we?"

"Silence." That one word, spoken temperately by his emperor, was enough to make the Herald straighten to attention as if a puppet on strings.

Sovereign had heard enough. He had stood there long enough. And he had tolerated this show to the extent of his ability.

Moving so fast it was a blur the wounded female's muddled vision would fail to follow, he put an end to the charade. One second he was across the room. Another, and his hand gripped Arden's shoulder, forcing the Herald away like a puppy tossed by its nape.

Sigil didn't have the strength to stop him, and he didn't have the heart to watch her bleed.

Collaring her throat in a careful grip, he removed the threat of jagged nails before she could cut herself any deeper. Sovereign made no move to force submission, even though he had her by the neck. Instead, he helped support her in the Herald's place.

He even tried to be reasonable. "What you propose, do you not see why it will cause discord in your life when what you need is consistency and peace?"

"You will give me Que." Eyes dyed a horrendous shade of purple, welled. She was so infinitely perfect to him even when utterly pathetic. He even had to laud how determined his Sigil was to control her shaking voice when she pleaded, "Prove that it is as you said. There need not be conflict between us."

Leaning nearer, Sovereign tried to reassure her, working to offer an impassive expression despite the surging fury he knew she could sense. "Can you feel my thoughts, Sigil? My answer to this ploy must be obvious."

Resting her head against the wall, sweat beading at her temples, she offered the only threat that might sway him. "Do you want to spend eternity wondering when I will find my next escape? That day will come. There is no perfect prison."

A thumb stroked along her jaw, Sovereign exercising great will to control his desperation to hold her. "If I offered such a consolation, you must understand that much will be expected in return. You will never show him affection. That shall be reserved only for your Brothers. You may not lie with him, ever." The thought that the Axirlan had already enjoyed her, that the alien had fucked her for decades, had Sovereign seeing red. Rage, jealousy, unfulfilled desire seeped into his expression. The emperor's every word came growled through clenched teeth, spat as if soaked in envy. "And for my forbearance, *you will love me.*"

He knew she found it an impossible request. Her fear was all there in the way she mewed at the word love, the way she trembled when he pressed closer.

Bloodshot eyes wide, vulnerable in a way that he longed to see in a more intimate scenario, his precious Sigil agreed. "I will, if..."

He'd give her anything if she would only keep looking at him with such eyes. "Yes?"

Sovereign waited for an explanation, and watched the strangest look of failure cross her face. "There is something else that I need."

His enthusiasm increased as she grew more pliant. Spoke with conviction, demanded, "Tell me what it is you need in exchange for your love."

She swallowed, seemed to consider, and then cast her gaze to the floor. "On storage deck H7, bulk 673, I have hidden a cryotube. The life inside it matters to me. If you swear to me the child will be removed from Pax and cared for, I will do what you want."

Sovereign turned her head so that he might look her in the eye again. "Who is this child?"

"A Tessan slave. I stole him."

"Sigil." A thumb stroked her jaw. He murmured her name as if she'd done something endearing and naughty. "I would have granted your request even if I had to carry you off the station in chains. See? I care for your feelings."

Quinn swayed, on the brink of unconsciousness. "You cannot wake him on the station or the collar will kill him."

"Understood."

"You swear to see to his freedom?" Sigil held out a grimy hand, in reference to human custom.

There was no hesitancy in taking the offered limb, but Sovereign did not shake it. He pressed a kiss to her palm instead, the man's face unflinching, his eyes brilliant. "The cryotube you speak of was taken into our custody several cycles ago. Deck H7, bulk 673 is where Arden reported he found you... collapsed over a sleeping child in the scrap heap registered for pickup by the Axirlan's ship."

Hearing that they had discovered her days before she'd begun to see the Herald in her shadow, that she had never really stood a chance... that they had captured Jerla, Sigil began to cry. "You would have hurt that boy, used him as a bargaining chip!"

"Shhhhhh. It didn't come to that." At once the emperor moved to soothe her anguish, gentle in tone, in touch. "In time, this knowledge will bring you comfort. You'll know that we loved you enough to assure we brought you home at any cost. You'll see our actions as assurances of that love, not as the threat that you imagine.

"I'll give you all that you want." Freeing her throat, his fingers trailing over her collar bones, he leaned down as if to kiss her. She braced, Sovereign paused, amending, "So long as you keep your word. Submit now. Show me you are willing."

Eyelids drooping, Sigil let him take his kiss.

Smiling, enraptured, Sovereign fussed over the female as if there had been no threats or fear. "Come, precious Sigil. Your wounds must be tended."

Her flagging bravado failed her when he lifted her to his chest. Intense pain from being jostled and she strained to be free of him.

It was no use.

Pinning her to the bed, Sovereign called for Karhl. The musical sound of chimes, tinkled as things were done to make their female very unhappy. The Lord Commander snapped a medical cuff around her arm, eliciting a shriek when contact caused thousands of microscopic fibers to burst from the device, penetrating into muscle and bone, making Sigil lurch and panic as they crawled deep into sinew and organs.

She'd tried to claw at it, to get it off, but the white behemoth had restrained the weakened woman with ease. "No, young one. Don't fight, and the discomfort of assimilation will decrease. There"—Karhl had stroked a tiny slice of exposed wrist, praising in a monotone when her spine gave and she ceased arching off the bed—"integration is almost complete."

While the med cuff did its work, her eyes screwed shut: so unlike a warrior and far more like a child. Even with her superior healing, the amount of decay the cuff syphoned from her body had been grotesque. Jars of black poison fed from tubes into the portable console, each emptied down the drain over and over so they might be refilled.

In one cycle, her fever broke. Sigil stopped raving in her sleep, and the woman convalescing altered significantly from the broken thing who had dared challenge an emperor, to an anguished captive who opened her mouth when told to. Who swallowed what was given.

A captive full of regret for falling for a pretty Herald's tricks.

The pompous Irdesian Empire had groveled perfectly while they scampered after their slippery prize. While it had been amusing—her game, how the human fools thought to outplay her—it had grown tiring. Drinta was angry now. It wasn't the flickering lights, or even the ruined water supply. It was their openness... the Empire's willingness.

They no longer skulked about, but instead wore their full dark raiment where others could see. They came to Swelter and partook. They enjoyed themselves openly, soldiers flaunting their meager numbers as if unconcerned they were surrounded.

Such behavior confused her agitated *guests*. The show convincing many of her summoned warriors there was a scheme between her and the Imperials. As if their easy smiles and haughty behavior were sanctioned. As if she had called the rabble horde to be offerings on Sovereign's pyre.

Subterfuge was *her* weapon and the Empire wielded it too well, bowing and scraping at her feet. Small minded human hubris never ceased to amaze, especially as it was so linear. The Empire was boring: take, convert, annihilate, repeat. Where was the artistry in so much tedium?

Were they wiser, they would follow her example: confuse, devour, decimate, enslave—all the while, being paid by each party involved.

"I have procured a present for you," the Tessan female crooned, an invitation in her black lidless eyes.

Smiling beautifully, Arden leaned back on his couch and teased, "I sincerely hope this story ends with you finding me a case of Tessan fire spirits."

She clicked her tongue and shook her head, light playing off glassy green scales. "No, no, no. Something much more interesting."

"And what would that be?" There was a glimmer in golden eyes—open, calculating assessment.

Drinta waved her hand before her, all sharp teeth and wicked beauty. "I'm getting to that. Patience. This is far too special to rush, let me savor..."

The golden male edged to the end of his seat, ignoring the squalor of Swelter at their feet. "My interest is piqued..."

"Good." She offered the playful laugh of an immoral woman. "But you'll have to wait a little longer. I find it far more enjoyable when I build suspense."

"In that case, I would like to admit that I have a surprise for you as well." There was a sweet quality to the tenor, something incredibly indulgent.

"Don't tease me, Arden." The tip of her tail gave a little swish. "You have no secrets from me."

Leaning his elbows on his knees, the emissary winked. "We've caught Sigil. Even now she is in Sovereign's clutches, chained, where he is urging her into tranquil submission. There will be no more disruptions to your station, and we are prepared to fully replace your water supply in honor of our fruitful alliance. Our apologies and gratitude will be profuse."

Easing back, comfortable, Drinta warned, "If you're trying to convince me to open the byway before repairs are finished, I am sorry, but no."

The man shook his head, golden eyes sparkling. "I wouldn't dream of it. Five days of her anger and Pax is near collapse. I can only imagine what the little terror did to the byway. It might be rigged to explode if opened. She wouldn't be above killing us all."

The Tessan laughed, an honest cackle full of teeth and zeal. "Is that her idea of going for the throat?"

"Not even close."

Chapter 15

If she lay still enough, slowed her thinking to a fine, focused point, it almost felt like Que was with her. Sovereign had taken over her rooms, set up his machines and his dominion, but he'd never bothered to change the bedding.

A teasing hint of Axirlan sweat drifted under her nose. The comfort that small taste of Que offered, how his scent still marked their bed, was keeping her sane.

Sane?

That concept was a joke now. Living in a constant state of psychosis had been manageable. Living with clarity was a nightmare.

And there was only one way Sovereign exercised the power to clear her mind of rampage, one way to make her meek.

Once he'd caught her, Sovereign had not missed a beat.

Quinn's attention shifted to the medical cuff uncomfortably engulfing the greater part of her forearm. Tubes filled with black matter syphoned from the apparatus, still drawing microscopic detritus into a field kit that purged infection. The fucking cuff had started healing her body, and without constant misery, it was less than an hour before her mind had shattered and full-blown bloodlust had rushed through the cracks.

The inevitability that he would fuck her again was part of their bargain. But the way in which it had been done…

Arden had delivered her on a silver platter, and the trio had been prepared. She'd fought their hold on her when they dragged her into her rooms. The invasion of the med cuff had sent her into convulsions, followed by fevered raving, followed by an overwhelming need to snuff out all life that had the audacity to creep near the suffering monster.

She fisted her hands so tightly that her knuckles cracked, that they'd shone white. All color bleached out of her vision until beautiful, perfect red remained—the red of Imperial blood she would paint the walls with.

The red of a long coming slaughter.

But there were hands on her, iron restraints.

Karhl had gripped her skull, so snapping teeth could not find their target. Despite the circling males, he'd forced her eyes to see nothing but the calmness of a warrior's face. Cheeks squished, spittle dripping from lips hissing horrific threats, Quinn had fought like a demon—a demon near death who lacked the strength to crawl away, let alone shift the weight of three strong Brothers.

The emperor stroked himself on the bed beside her. Tugging at his cock, the menacing organ grew angry and swollen in his hands. Meanwhile, Arden pinned her legs, while Karhl dared to promise that they would make it quick.

The harder she fought their hold, the greater her insanity grew.

When her psionics began to flare, the emperor spread her thighs and crawled between them.

Pain came. Sovereign's bulbous glans slipped its way just past her unprepared opening, her swollen belly protesting invasion. Sheer agony snapped her free of the worst of the madness, stopped the cycling psionics, and made her recognize what was being done. She tried to tell them that it was enough, that the pain could keep her sane, that they didn't have to do this.

Wheezing, coughing up blood, she told them to stop.

Not one of them answered her croaking denial.

Sovereign never fucked into her. In the horrible minutes it took for him to come, his pumping fist supplied the friction necessary for male climax. He even had the civility to keep quiet when the only thing that would truly sedate her raving ushered forth.

Warmth, a thing that smelled of the ocean and stuck like glue, spurted like ointment straight into her body. What came in the wake of the unwanted offering, she wished it would have killed her.

Despair, humiliation, disgust.

They ate at her mind in a way the madness never had

"I should never have listened to your lying Herald!" She'd screwed her eyes shut as if that would make them disappear. "It would have been better had I died trying to be free."

"Hush, young one." Karhl had gripped her skull in his great hands, forced her attention as if it had just been the two of them, not three predators moving in unison. "We could not allow you to exercise faulty psionics in a panic. Your life was in danger."

How she longed to spit in his face.

Clawing at the sheets, she'd dragged them over her dirty, naked body, and tried to disappear. Curled up on the very bed she'd shared with Que for almost a decade, she stared at the ceiling, at the walls, at anything but the other lifeforms in the room, limp from illness and ennui.

When she sobbed, she hardly cared that they stood witness.

After all, what dignity did she have left?

Sovereign traced the line of Sigil's spine, bone by bone down her bare back. Fingertips flared each time he reached her more tempting curves, as if memorizing their softness. Then his stroke reversed, bottom to nape, the continuation of touch running an unhurried course.

Lounging at her back, he feigned laziness, unwilling to let his guard down no matter how complacent his Consort might appear. Every breath she took, he counted, each little twitch scrutinized with a hawk's eye.

He put his lips to her nape, sucked softly, giving her something else to think on other than her open obsession: *Que*.

That was the name she called out for over and over when her fever was at its worst—an emotionless alien who'd kept her like a pet, who had whored her out in Swelter for cash... who had allowed a slave collar to circle her perfect throat.

It was Sovereign she should have been calling for. After all, he had loved her from first sight. Conquered the humans for her. Adored her. Suffered a century of loneliness.

What could an Axirlan know of love?

Sigil would learn. The Brotherhood would charm her, adore her until the alien was forgotten—until her whole world was only him, his Brothers, their children, all existing in harmony.

Prepared to be patient, overjoyed to finally have her near, Sovereign rolled her to her back and stared down at the naked creature caught in his arms.

The tears had stopped hours ago. Her pallor faded until life had returned to pinken her skin.

Leaning down to breathe her in, he moved slowly, cautiously, so she wouldn't startle.

He didn't need to be an empath to know the woman was still very upset and questioning her surrender, though she hid it behind an impassive expression.

Sigil was his now. Her fragile mental and physical state had improved. And with her Tessan boy his hostage and their shaky agreement concerning the Axirlan in place, Sovereign had her firmly in his grip.

It would take time for his precious Sigil to learn to trust him, he understood that. He whispered so in her ear each time her shivering beckoned him to draw nearer to warm her. "It may not feel instinctive now, but I promise you, my love, it will become more natural than breathing. We were designed for one another."

She'd made a sound like retching.

He settled his weight nearer. "We had an agreement, Sigil."

She refused to answer. Refused to look at him, speak to him, or acknowledge his hand on her flesh… even if it meant displaying her vulnerable nape when she turned away.

He'd already subdued her rage, filled her with his seed, and crooned over her as she curled in on herself afterward. Time had been given to recover, comfort had been offered. He'd bathed the dried blood and sweat from her skin himself. Tended each wound.

But the reprieve was over. Now he wanted her attention.

A warm palm flowed over her and gently cradled her healed belly. "Sweet Sigil, everything that was done can be undone. I swear it to you. Desolation is unnecessary."

Apparently, he had said the right words to draw out a reply.

She spoke for the first time since he'd corrected her conditioning. But her voice and spirit were flat. "If such a thing were possible, it would have been undone a long time ago. Just like you, I'm a monster, Sovereign. I can admit to what I am."

The emperor disagreed. "Is that what the Axirlan told you?"

"Yes, and Que was right." Frustration, disgust, and hope twisted together in her words. "He's dedicated his life to helping me cage that nightmare, so it might not pollute the undeserving. But I always slip. I have done things, massacred innocents... I know what I'm capable of, and not one bit of it is good."

Sovereign looked into her eyes, very pleased to see all the lavender dye had been drained away by the med cuff and left them the crystalline blue he favored. "What about the Tessan boy you stole? Your motivation there would say differently."

"My plans for Jerla are none of your business."

"But you wanted him kept safe, didn't you?" The back of his fingers stroking her cheek, he whispered, "You *are* capable of compassion."

The woman snapped, batting his hand away. "How much longer must we stay here? I'm well. Confining me to my bed is pointless now... so why isn't the station vibrating? Why isn't the byway open?"

Sovereign stretched as if to shield her view of anything but him. He smiled sweetly at her frowns, he tried to adore. "I enjoy speaking with you."

"You promised me Que. You promised me Jerla. Produce them or get off of me!"

Running his nose up her neck, he murmured, "You're doing well, Sigil. You've been patient, but we both know why we are still here in this room."

She had the audacity to sneer.

Sovereign rubbed himself against her so she might feel what was on offer. "You must be prepared. *Completely stable*. When you are ready for me, I will be gentle. I will show you sex between us does not need to be horrific, or painful, or frightening. Afterward, we'll go to Drinta together, where I am going to present you and kill her for all of Swelter to witness."

An angry red crept over Sigil's cheeks. Her eyes, devoid of the purple dye, shone bright and wrathful. That anger died as soon as it was born. She blinked, turned her gaze away, and almost chuckled. "Only Drinta has the power to open the byway. If she's dead, you're stranded. And I don't think the uppity Empire will take to Pax as well as I did. You all look so clean all the time."

Sovereign's smirk was pure evil, somewhat playful, and extremely hungry. "You haven't seen us at war."

"You can't kill Drinta." Each word was spoken with inflection, with the harsh reality of the situation Sigil painstakingly explained. "The byway is keyed to her living body. Everyone knows that! If she dies, it will not function. By the time you got it back online, Pax would be beyond repair. The warring factions trapped here would destroy it fighting to claim the prize."

"The byway was rekeyed shortly after we first spoke."

Scoffing, Sigil shook her head. "To you?"

His attempted seduction was over. Rearing up so she might see just how serious he was, Sovereign said, "No. I'm ultimately expendable. It was rekeyed to you. You are more important than anything in the universe."

His words did not have the desired effect. His consort only grew angry. Leaning up on her elbows, she met his intensity with a hiss of her own. "Then why isn't it open?"

"It still requires a command code. A specific action, if you will. Deauthorization of the original keyholder."

"You have got to be kidding me…" The brand of horror on her face was almost cute. "I sat there, right in front of her AND ALL I NEEDED TO DO WAS KILL HER TO GET OUT?"

"Sigil, if you think we would have made it that easy for you, you've failed to understand how much you matter to us." A kiss, simple and non-threatening Sovereign pressed to Sigil's shoulder. He began to caress, to ease her back down against the mattress. "Her enclosure is fortified, the safest place on this station. Drinta must die, and you must be on the dais when it's done. Before any faction might seek to grab power, I will then open the byway. The Imperial fleet will be through it in an instant, we will be collected, and Pax will fall under my control."

Sigil pushed up from the pillows again, laughing right in his face. "You cannot be so arrogant. The Tessan Authority will never allow you to control an extended byway on the other side of their empire. It would start an intergalactic war."

Sovereign's internal pleasure that she had engaged, that she even risked putting her hand on his bared chest inspired a low groan. Forced to catch himself, he steadied his breath and answered, "The politics are far more complicated than we have time to discuss at present."

"And just what will you do to Pax?"

Fingers reached out to play with the lobe of her ear, Sovereign easing ever closer. "Pax is to be converted into something more useful to me."

The moment was ruined by her instant regret. In fact, she sounded heartbroken. "You can't convert non-humans."

"I know you are fond of this place, the same cannot be said for the majority of the lives who inhabit it. I have watched you kill on a whim with no thought for whose neck you snapped. You have no friends here. Even the slaves were avoided." He wanted to reignite her interest in debate, to entice her to engage… to touch him again. "I understand why you did these things. I understand what pushed you to the point of living in a state of constant violence. Once you're back in the Empire—"

"With Que..." Sigil insisted.

Doing his best to control the angry tick in his jaw, Sovereign continued as if the interruption had not taken place. "Once you are back in the Empire, you will know what it means to feel safe. There will be no urge for you to hide, no overwhelming impulse you have to fight. The drastic change in your environment will alter your responses. You will be happy."

"I was happy here..."

Eyes absolutely burning, he stated a hard truth. "You do not know what that word means, and your alien lacked the empathy to teach it to you. All you know is 'pain' or 'no pain' in a stunted understanding of survival."

Sovereign had witnessed hours of Sigil's struggle to keep the dread out of her expression. He knew their female already second-guessed her decision to obey. And in that moment, all he saw was rebellion—rebellion in her slander, in her unhappiness about what was to be done to her home... rebellion in her look of hate. "You are beginning to sound as verbose as Arden, but not nearly as subtle."

"I raised Arden, trained him." A small quirk came to the corner of Sovereign's beautiful mouth. "I think, in time, you will find it quite the other way around. He copies my mannerisms and intonation almost to perfection."

"Why?"

Possessiveness ate at the softness of his reply. "Because you were designed to respond to *me*—

chemically, physically, mentally. Mimicry simplified interrogation." Gently, Sovereign pressed his fingers to her mouth when it looked like the woman might argue again. "And now you are thinking he has fooled you, suspicion is all over your face. But you are wrong, and I will prove it now. The bite." He watched her blanch, felt Sigil wilt as if it might keep her spine safe from his teeth. "You claimed to hate it. But the truth is you fear it. Like a child's fear of ghosts, you jump at every touch, anticipating this thing you misunderstand."

When he moved to turn her skull and expose her weak point, the whites of her eyes shone stark around abnormally pale irises.

"I will not bite you so long as you continue to submit in good faith." In counter to his claim, Sovereign slid his hand to cup her neck, pinching lightly, watching as her body twitched and her knees jerked just enough for him to comprehend the effect. "It is a very generous offer."

The smile he gave her, the way it slowly crawled up his cheeks, was saturated in conceit. "Do you understand? Do you not see that I would rather suffer than see you afraid or sad? The thought of your hate has burned me for a century. I do not wish to earn more of it."

His pinch between the bones grew stronger, Quinn suffering the effect as Sovereign meant for her to feel it. He kissed her brow sweetly, released her, and said, "Our pairings have not been pleasant for you, but you enjoyed the feeling of Karhl's hands and mouth while I fucked you. I can give you that.

Imagine more. Imagine four, ten, of our kind, their lips and hands teasing your body. Imagine the way we'll taste, how greedy each will be to earn your smiles. Or…" He took her lips, groaning as he ran his tongue over the seam. "Imagine you and I alone in the dark. Imagine how I could worship you, the pleasure of the struggle."

A deep breath of her neck and he shuddered, grinding hips to demonstrate intent. "You won't understand right away—I grasp that—but I will make you want me more than any other. Desire, pleasure. We shall start simply." In a fluid movement, Sovereign stroked her leg from ankle to hip. "But for now we must make the best of things. Trust me to keep you safe and allow me to prepare you. I cannot have you slip in Drinta's presence. Spread your legs for me. I'll be gentle."

Chapter 16

Her last cry was wrung out until she convulsed, Quinn sloppy atop her damp sheets.

Sovereign's skilled handling of her body was the worst kind of intoxicant, surpassing even *lupggag*, the exotic hallucinogenic drug bartered in Swelter. Nose tucked in the man's dark hair, her breath grew drenched in a strangely familiar scent. A smell that quieted her brain to the point where dread never existed, and nothing was left beyond the physical—his weight, the breadth of his hips spreading her thighs, the feel of what plunged inside her, all-consuming, tempting her tongue to trace over the pulsing vein at his throat.

How he'd bent her body back after that first lick, how he'd growled. Sovereign had been so pleased.

Her clit ached from too much attention. It was stiff and swollen, pert enough to be tormented each time Sovereign thrust in a downward scrape of movement that purposefully targeted that flesh.

"Please..."

"Gods yes, Sigil." Another slow, measured intrusion of the man's veiny dick pushed deeper.

Again he dug into her mouth with his tongue.

If orgasm could last into infinity, Quinn found it was not a sensation physically bearable. The grunting, panting man who watched her every expression offered too much—either too slow or too fast. Somewhere under the onslaught, that tiny sliver of cognizance almost longed for him to bite her, for the man to pound until his sack tightened and he spurt, ending the obliterating fucking she'd endured.

Had it been days or hours? Quinn could hardly say.

Her nipples chafed from having been sucked too long, the flesh sore from a flicking tongue and pinching fingers. Once or twice she thought Karhl's mass might have been between them to lull the storm, but that cock had never left her, and even though Sovereign's possession had been cautious, it had never been gentle in the way the white-haired warrior touched her.

Worse, the maelstrom inside Sovereign was beyond her reckoning, His emotions were overwhelming. So she tried not to sense him, engaging instead to prove she deserved her coming prize. He could have her if she could have Que—who would never have fucked her once her pussy ached. Who would never have squeezed further pleasure from swollen lips and a hardened, punished clit. He would have pressed her to sleep. But Sovereign, Sovereign punished for such thoughts by breaking her apart, nerve by nerve.

Past coherent words, Quinn spoke in tongues, made any sound she thought her aggressor might find suiting in his quest to be begged—because it had to end. A rougher grind, and his hips crashed into her. Her poor pierced clit took the brunt of the abuse and Quinn sought to fight back.

That was what the man had searched for, that utter loss of control, the mindless wash of her eyes. He fed her madness with violence, taking and intruding deep into body and spirit. The invasion of his cock grew frantic, his lips returning to her bobbing breast to roughly chew a tender nipple.

Her screams shrilled otherworldly until Quinn's voice broke, as did the waste of worried thoughts hovering at the edge of her mind. Her hand flashed forward, Sovereign's throat in her grip. Somehow he was beneath her—like their battle cycles prior—and she furiously rode him, her circling hands squeezing his neck so hard it would have killed even Que. Relishing the sight of her tormentor so fucking pleased, so goddamn delirious, she came, gushing as he smiled.

There was some pull—a strange thing she missed—and she was flipped on her back. The man jerked violently into her as he locked her violence in loving arms. With a filthy groan, Sovereign's cock spit ropes of burning perfection into her greedy little pussy.

Disheveled and hungry, lying on a bed that had grown damp from sweat, Quinn stared at the ceiling. Another spasm hit her, her body trembling awkwardly just from the feel of Sovereign easing out.

Panting, she whined. "No more."

"No more, sweet Sigil." The lightest of kisses landed on each pebbled nipple. "You cannot handle any more."

They had both been so lost in the oblivion of coitus, a part of her had wondered if their cries would call forth Drinta's overseers. Her tiny sliver of hope the bitch-queen would use the advantage to kill the Irdesian emperor in his distraction was disappointed.

Salvation had not come, only orgasm after orgasm, the man seeming never to tire as he wrung her out.

Fingers tripped over her skull, the touch drawing out a relaxation so thorough Quinn put up no fight when she was pulled to her feet. The oddity of what had happened was reinforced when her muddled mind found the emperor naked on display. Every other time he had fucked her, it had been a clinical necessity in comparison—his clothing had remained on, his cock jutting out from an open fly to serve as the tool required to control her compulsion.

There had been no objective insertion and ejaculation, no hurried spurt inside her, proven when Sovereign took his time over the last hours, mounting her face to face. He'd left her boneless and rubbery. Exhausted her into a state all would recognize when she was paraded before Drinta.

She looked cowed, resplendent in her abject defeat.

What a trophy for Swelter to gawk at.

When she'd been fevered, the emperor had sponged the dried blood from her skin—the nearest thing to a bath she was going to find on a station infected with irradiated water. Now she reeked of Sovereign, thighs gritty where their fluids had crusted and smeared. Purposefully made that way so others might see.

Sovereign insisted on dressing her, Quinn standing submissive so the process might proceed. Stranger still, they were left alone, no guard in sight, a thousand things within reach she could make into a weapon.

She chewed the nutrient bar he'd offered her, watching the man begin the task of unrolling a bolt of fabric, and sensed no suspicion—only warranted wariness and determination.

Holding out a corner of fabric, Sovereign pressed it to the dip above her hip bone and ordered, "Hold here."

Obeying, she watched him build a gown around her. It was an intricate thing requiring so many steps, so much precision, her clothing would make a humiliating statement. Only a prisoner meek and obedient could be dressed in such a delicately constructed manner. Only one who was completely controlled.

A finger hooked her chin, Sovereign tilting her head back to soothe her frowns. "I viewed a sunset once, on the planet Yith-ji, over a battlefield where the corpses of my enemies were growing entwined with carnivorous plant life. The shade of the sky was just as this." A finger teased at the fringe of Quinn's lashes, Sovereign cooing, "I put the beauty of that moment in you."

Quinn had not seen herself, but it was not hard to imagine what Sovereign spoke of. The eyes she was born with stared back at him now that the tint had been drained away by the damned medical cuff: a dark limbal ring, irises a limpid shade rare in humans.

They were not eyes one could hide, designed and unnatural. They had always set her apart.

Where he found pleasure, she felt nothing. Her looks had never held meaning to her outside of their inconvenient noticeability—just like the clothing he'd brought from the Empire to knot and wrap and twist around her.

Another swath of airy fabric was draped across her breasts, whatever hooks or ties Sovereign employed to attach it hidden. The forming garment lacked the Imperial black the men wore, just shades of blue in a dress so intricate it was pointless in its grandeur, utterly different in style from the red beaded gown she'd destroyed, and no less ridiculous.

A broach was pinned between her breasts to hold the layers snug. Tracing her finger over the jewelry's needle, a thing long and thick enough to kill a man if used properly, she muttered, "Is all of this to shame me as your tamed conquest?"

Sovereign gave the final belt a tug, and everything fell into place.

The challenge in his eyes did not match the set of his lips. "Considering the trouble you have caused Drinta, I cannot dress you in armor without drawing her suspicion. Seeing you subdued and non-threatening will amuse her and serve my agenda."

Quinn would have rather been naked than paraded, used, and ornamented. "Do convert women dress this way?"

Sovereign cracked a hint of a smirk, lifting the final, sleeveless vestment so she might slip her arms into it. "The females have distinct customs this gown reflects—complication, for one. The elite do not dress themselves."

Tracing the embroidered birds in flight adorning the floor-length vest, the stiffness of something weighty over so many panels of gauzy blues, Quinn asked, "To display rank?"

"Lineage, taste, power. It is an art beyond itself at court that seems to please a great many of them."

She'd never seen such a thing from the Empire. "But you and your Brothers only wear black. The soldiers wear black. Irdesian armor is black..."

Sorrow and matching coldness sat heavy in Sovereign's gaze. "We have been in mourning. We lost what we loved most."

She sensed his deeper feelings, a dark thing inside him hidden by a soldier's protocol. "You are very angry with me."

Sovereign shook his head, but he didn't touch her to reassure as had been his habit. "My anger is for Commander Dimitri and those who took you from me."

No matter what he claimed, he harbored resentment. She could feel it. "You could have been free of me a long time ago. You could have left me in peace."

"Abandoning you to indifference was never an option." He took a step back to survey his work, their line of conversation over. "You look very beautiful..."

Under so much finery she felt absurd.

"...and unsure." He reached for her. "Take my hand and I will lead you home."

It was so similar to what Arden had said to her that it made her stomach flip.

Quinn swallowed and the anxious stutter in her heart doubled when he subtly flicked his fingers. Yet hope burned, just enough to make her worry even more. It was a waste of emotion hoping Drinta might actually win, that there might still be some small chance at escape in the ensuing chaos. But that would put Que at risk from one side or another. The Empire would hunt him down given the chance, and should Drinta know his tie to her, she too would reach out her claws and revenge herself upon him for Quinn's part in her troubles.

By failing to flee Pax, Quinn had inadvertently created a situation where she had to side with the Empire. Once it was open, Sovereign would take the station and control the byway. She would even help if she had to. She would help for Que. And if all went well, she would have him back in a matter of cycles.

Together they would scheme their way out of this mess and run far far away from Sovereign, his Brothers, and the Empire.

That was how it had to be. Quinn couldn't be a part of Pax any longer. It was too tight, too dry. It had cast her off like a serpent shedding its skin.

So, she took Sovereign's outstretched hand, clammy fingers settled into a firm grip. "Que is my home. Take me anywhere, so long as he is there."

Sovereign had the decency to pet her fingers, to bend down and press a soft kiss to nervous lips. "Recognize that I did not chain you. This is your chance to prove yourself honorable to our pact."

The walk—no, the procession—to Swelter was a joke of decorum. As if bleeding from the walls, Imperial soldiers formed a cocoon about them, she the butterfly trapped inside. They were a show, a cavalcade of black, holstered weapons, and pride before the gangs haunting the sprawling club.

The infamous Lord Commander Karhl walked point like a threatening banner. No less than twenty of Sovereign's elite-convert humans finalized the ranks—ten thousand of the worse spacer-scum gawking as they moved by.

They had the attention of the entire hive, save one lone female sheltered at the center of the grouping. Quinn found her attention pulled elsewhere. She stared at the distant red swath of silk she'd twisted in for the last ten years. Already another slave performed in her place, as if it had never been hers at all.

Pax would have already forgotten about the plum-haired slave, her replacement beautiful and drawing her own crowd. And all those looking, the species watching the Imperial Consort in the rainbow of blues whispering around her legs, would not have known she'd ever been one of them.

It hurt.

Sovereign handed her up to the final platform, Karhl at her back, his hand on her shoulder before the large floor elevated the party to Drinta's balcony. The bitch-queen stood, beautiful and deadly, a mismatched collection of the universe's most vicious mercenaries at her back.

Had Quinn any interest in watching the proceedings, she would have laughed at the show, wondering at the money and promises it had taken to get the thug, Lhhuy, to stand beside the rival gang leader, Ved.

Sovereign brushed her cheek, showing her the liquid gathered on his fingers. "It's almost over, Sigil."

She didn't acknowledge his words, her attention still tripping over the club as if she stared at an unfaithful lover.

He pressed a kiss to her temple, but Sovereign's eyes were full of something dark, staring straight at Drinta, who chortled as he fawned obnoxiously over his pet.

Arden, standing beside the Mistress of Pax, greeted his liege. "Emperor Sovereign, Imperial Consort Sigil, Lord Commander Karhl. Welcome."

The balcony was cramped and ripe for quite a mess. And there was hardly a reason for Quinn to admit what she sensed, any creature wise enough to know fire was hot could see it. Still, she did her part to prove herself. Whatever it took to get to Que. "Drinta is going to try to kill you, Sovereign."

The emperor chuckled, bowing to the Mistress of Pax. "You give her too little credit, Sigil."

"Sovereign." The black lidless eyes darted towards the unsmiling Sigil and began to glitter. Drinta looked as if she might reach out and touch the wayward slave. She even dared to take a step forward. "Your reluctant queen... cowed I see... but not chained as Arden claimed she would be."

"Oh, do not doubt it. Sigil is dangerous. Lord Commander Karhl has leave to execute her should she move." Releasing Quinn's hand, Sovereign bowed so deeply it was almost insulting. "But that is not my greatest concern. I understand you have charmed my Herald from me."

Drinta swept her hands from shoulder to shoulder in her species most respectful greeting. "He lies. But he does so with such a pretty mouth."

Sovereign conceded her point. "He is quite popular..."

Needle sharp teeth exposed, Drinta looked to Quinn, still finding no more than a profile and obnoxious dress offered for her perusal. "Quinn, former Pax slave, now Consort of the Irdesian Empire. Seeing you like this, I almost regret I did not give you what you wanted."

Liar. Drinta's motivations were so easy to sense it was a joke. Scoffing, Quinn looked away from the club to focus again on the green Tessan. "Not nearly so much as I do, bitch-queen."

Looking to Sovereign, Drinta sang, "I do believe she threatened me."

"Mistress Drinta," Sovereign stepped in front of Quinn as if to shield the Mistress of Pax from his prisoner. "She did."

"Am I allowed to enjoy her for it?" Drinta trilled, tail languidly moving like a serpent at her back.

"Pax is yours. You are allowed to do whatever you please."

Tuning out the verbal sparring, thick compliments, and general disgusting back and forth, Quinn turned her back to their politics and leaned just enough on Karhl so he would not suspect she might try to break the energy barrier separating the balcony from the club and flee.

Immediately, the Lord Commander set a hand to her hip, fingers enveloping the bone. He pulled her flush, his chin resting casually atop her head.

Quinn hardly noticed, too keen on the fact her hand skimmed a weapon holstered at the Lord Commander's thigh. It was all she could to do focus on the pulsing music and restrain herself from fingering the deadly piece—imaginings of pulling it free, of shooting Sovereign, Karhl, Arden, and all the others so pretty and so nauseating in their current invincibility, distracting.

She thought of Que, looking to their favorite places to enjoy one another in the club's more interesting corners.

"As I mentioned to your enjoyably duplicitous Herald—"

Arden was only happy to speak over her. "Your compliments are too elegant, Drinta."

"—I have a gift I am eager to offer. First it was intended to please Arden. A fruit plucked for offering almost the very day we met. However, I have since learned that your Herald is disgustingly loyal. What he desired was not for himself, it was for you, Sovereign. And so I give it to you with all my heart." The bitch-queen turned wistful, her voice blending with the sluggish susurration of cloth being pulled. "Now I see how much more valuable this trophy is. The conversations we had after he denied my incredibly generous offer for one pleasure slave's purchase... Would you believe he even tried to warn me? He called your pretty terrorist an abomination. I believe he told her his name was Que."

"No!"

At the sound of that name, Quinn looked away from the club, right at the prepared *gift*. Like a whore raising her skirts, the final bit of cloth dragged over a cube shaped object displayed between the two parties, falling until all Quinn could hear was a scream so shrill she was certain her ears bled.

Even if she had not seen, she would have felt it in the dread of the minds of the three sheep—the men already responding, already trying to intervene...

because they too had seen and they were ripe with fear.

The passage of time slowed to a drip. Quinn heard Sovereign as if he stood across a sea, shouting, "Calm yourself, Sigil!"

Calm? She *was* calm.

Feeling the slickness of ocular tissue shift in their sockets, the slow drag of eyeball against lid, Sigil looked over a horror: her lovely Que's head displayed battered in a cryobox—staring forward, eyes flat, lids uneven. His familiar mouth slightly agape, Que was lovely no more.

A distant screech of wailing, a furious storm of grief and groaning metal seemed to mourn along with the earsplitting sound of sobs.

"SIGIL, STOP YOURSELF!"

But it was too late...

In the end, no one was as strong as she. And she proved it in a flick of the wrist and another irrepressible burst of dangerous psionics. The tremors grew, Swelter alight with sparks of blue energy she ripped from atoms, throwing everyone in that alcove so ferociously bones shattered on impact. All but one. Three steps and the Tessan female, Drinta, her muzzle one of shock, looked upon what Quinn really was.

"Where is the rest of my Que?" That voice, it was the voice of nightmares—a broken voice.

Drinta watched entire portions of Swelter rip away from their supports to fall, crashing against twisting artificial gravity. "Look at them behind you.

How frantic they are, and how easily broken by one barren human. Sovereign, even Karhl, cannot break through your barrier, can they?"

"WHERE. IS. HE?"

Below them, the mob surged, madness broke out as slaves and mercenary screamed and fled the destruction.

As beautifully as Drinta's plan unfolded, it also crashed in on her. Already Swelter's walls were opening to space, atmosphere leaking away. Haughty, looking into eyes vacant of control, Drinta faced death with a sneer. "Ask the right question... but you can't, can you?" The Tessan grinned. "Ask why."

Why? Because Arden had recognized her in the club and Drinta had noticed. It was that terrible and that simple.

Que had never left Pax... his altered exit schedule nothing but an easy trap to draw him aside the second he seemed relatively useful. And all that time Quinn had sought him, he'd been right there. She could have saved him, and failed. The Tessan had already hinted as much.

"Why?"

"Because I could. Because he and my Kilactarin both warned me to kill you. But I will offer you your life instead if you kill Sovereign. We could align ourselves, you and I, delightful human. I will get you another pet, a more loyal Axirlan, if you desire it."

Movement almost lazy, Quinn's hand stretched through the electric storm. Drinta twitched, unable to move from the psionic restraint one paltry human manifested. Not that the Tessan didn't try. She thrashed until her arm broke and bone jutted from the wound.

Brushing the center of Drinta's chest, Quinn's fingers slowly rent flesh, the reptile struggling for the strength to hiss. "You would dare deny me?"

Quinn's fingertips jammed forward, crushing through cartilage, breaching a reptilian chest cavity in search of a thumping organ similar to a human heart. Her fist closed on that erratically beating mass and tore it from Drinta's chest. Holding it up so the bitch-queen might see it, she crushed that gelatinous tissue in her fist.

As the bitch-queen's eyes went dark, Quinn wrapped her grip around the Tessan's jaw. With a burst of inhuman power, Quinn ripped Drinta's pretty head off its pretty, glittering shoulders.

"SIGIL, YOU MUST CALM DOWN!"

There was that pesky negation again, that sad attempt to bend her psionics and tug her back. But Quinn was too busy stomping the fresh corpse into a pulp under her feet.

Walls warped, and the energy barriers on Drinta's balcony failed. The shutters fell, some broken, their protection failing. Layers of force fields distorted from Quinn's flares. Even with backup canisters of gas releasing new air to counter the loss of atmosphere, breath was hard to find.

Death was coming, Quinn's rage the reaper of them all.

Sobbing, she left the gooey mass of green fluid and shattered bone, tripping to fall atop her friend. Wrapping her arms around the cryobox, she screamed and screamed, tearing what little remained of Pax apart in an unadulterated surge of violent psionics. There was no stopping it. Her mind stretched a thousand places at once, damaging her as it ravaged the station. Whole pieces broke off in the tumult of energy flares, thousands of lives lost in a blink as the vacuum of space invaded.

Draped over her friend's skull, blood came from her ears, her nose.

Sovereign was shouting for her, the man trapped, trying to break through her barrier.

But it was far from enough

Atmosphere leaked from the fragmented remains of Swelter, the fortified alcove's shields failing from her assault. Gravity disappeared, and still she sobbed.

It would be over soon. Quinn could already feel the lack of air bringing with it a dimness of consciousness to ease so much pain.

In one sad shuddering exhale, breath left her body, the dark overcoming a brain already hemorrhaging and a heart that hurt so badly she would have ripped it out of her own chest had she any strength left.

Chapter 17

Alarms blared. The shielded alcove of a dead felon-queen hissed with the escape of necessary air. Sovereign fought to reach for Sigil, who floated limp and spent in the chaos she'd created. Her psionics had failed right before the third set of backup tanks kicked in. Lost atmosphere was replaced in the disintegrating balcony, Karhl and Arden systematically ensuring all Drinta's peons were crushed into dust.

Pax was lost, had burst apart like a wasps' nest fallen from a tree. The byway, however, had come online the instant Sovereign had given the command—the instant Sigil had ripped out Drinta's heart.

The station was in ruins. From their shielded alcove all around them, open space was visible from huge gaping rents the manic female had torn into the walls. Outside their failing shell, Sigil's instantaneous attack had caused a panic at the docks. Ships could be seen dodging chunks of debris, trying to flee through the gate even as the Imperial fleet invaded.

Every foreign shuttle was obliterated without question or offer of surrender.

"How did intel of this level slip through your fingers?" The rage in Sovereign as he held Sigil's blood-soaked, body was beyond anything Arden had witnessed.

The Herald looked at the female, took in the red drips running from her ears, nose, and mouth. "I knew Drinta had detained the Axirlan the moment it happened."

Karhl struck him first, breaking the weaker Brother's cheek in one hard crack. "You forget your place!"

His reply was muddled, Arden holding the bones of his jaw in place so he might answer. "It had to be done this way. You had to be innocent of any part in it. Sigil could never be allowed to keep him. It would tempt her to run or divide her loyalty as time wore on."

Had Sigil not been in his grip, Sovereign would have ended one of his most trusted Brothers in that very moment. "So you took it upon yourself to damage her."

Tears leaked from golden eyes, a grimace on his face when Karhl systematically broke both his shoulders. The Herald looked upon the woman he loved. "She will survive it. Pax had to be cleansed. No one could know where she came from or what she'd been. Considering how damaged she already was, a clean start is in our power now. I willingly sacrifice myself for such a boon to our people. I did this for you—for her."

There was no question of punishment. Incapacitated as Arden was, having been brought to his knees by Karhl's continuous precise snap of bones, the Herald had eyes only for the bleeding woman, and said, "I wanted to give you the best possible chance."

Sovereign turned his attention away from such a great disappointment. "Kill him."

One sickeningly fast downward punch twisted Arden's neck until pleading eyes could no longer look at the one he'd betrayed.

Boot lifted to crush Arden's skull, to finish it, Karhl prepared to end it.

But Sovereign stopped him with a soft spoken word. "Wait."

Foot braced to strike, Karhl looked at the crumpled body of his Brother. Stone-cold, he growled, "Arden betrayed us. He deviated from the plan to follow his own agenda. Why spare the traitor?"

Arden's twisted form still breathed even after so much damage; he would survive if left as he was. Contemplating the fallen Herald, Sovereign sighed. "I have a greater punishment in mind for Arden."

It was rare for disgust to infest Karhl's inflection. "You may have raised him, but he does not deserve your pity."

"And he will receive none. Arden will be denied ever having her in any connotation deeper than one of Brotherhood. Such castigation will be a lifelong sentence worse than any prison. He will never be allowed to court one of her daughters."

The Lord Commander did not agree. "If he should survive, do you really believe a secret of this magnitude can be permanently concealed from an empath?"

Even damaged, she was so beautiful cradled on his lap. Sovereign traced over her temple, over where her brain was firing improperly to the point her face twitched. "If he wishes to live, he will employ his greatest talent and manipulate her trust. Sigil is fond of him. When she wakes she'll desire a friend. He will sit with her, act as her guide, and never be anything more."

The great maw of the nearest warship opened, particle traction slipping around their failing enclosure. In seconds, the balcony was in the belly of the vessel's cargo bay. Minutes later, Sigil was laid in cryo, still soaked in the green slime of her last kill.

Thank you for reading Sigil! I hope you loved our darling psychopath and the men who adore her! Read SOVEREIGN now! Full chapter teaser ahead.

Sign up for my newsletter 🐾

http://bit.ly/AddisonCainNewsletter

Now, please enjoy an extended excerpt of SOVEREIGN...

SOVEREIGN

Part Two of the Irdesi Empire Series

Waves breaking against rocks and the crisp rumble of vast water stole through dreams of ripping metal and hissing gasses. It was not easy to wake, to find that each breath smelled slightly of salt and not of stale recycled atmosphere.

Brightness muddled sight when lashes parted and Sigil found the proverbial vision of heaven.

The side of her face pressed to cloth the same color as Que's flesh. Facing open gates of glass that offered blue sky, she felt nothing but the torments of hell. A growing sob crushed her heart, and she shut her eyes so tight her skull ached.

Long ago, before her name was Quinn, she had cried like that—like a dying animal. Alone, cut off from sentient life after she'd eaten the last of her attackers on that wild world she'd crashed into as a child. There she'd howled pitifully after ages of solitude.

That same horrible emptiness hollowed her out now.

The only life that mattered to her was lost.

There was no Que to guide her. She'd been deserted, left in a palatial room with walls that glowed as if carved from opal. There was no Que because his battered head had been cut off and placed in a cryobox.

There was no Que because she had utterly failed him.

This was all her fault.

Her cries distorted into muffled screams against the soft foreign mattress, each breath more painful than any blow she'd ever taken. Howls built until she could hardly breathe, until the pressure behind her eyes brought piercing pain to her skull.

Blood dripped from her nostrils. She ignored it. After all, the covers had already grown damp from her outburst. The whole of that great bed may as well have been broken glass.

Quinn bawled until there were no more tears.

The subsequent exhausted numbness deadened a bit of the grief.

Staring dumbly out those huge open doors to a balcony drenched in sun, she willed her heart to stop beating.

Her body denied her. Sleep came instead.

The next time she woke, what had been almost blinding whiteness had altered to soft gold sunlight. Aching as if she'd slept too long, hungry, confused, she pressed up from the vast bed.

Her wrists were circled by etched gold, the bracelets' decoration of ancient design jingled when she moved. Her nails had been shaped, cleaned. There was no crust of dried blood on her face or grainy remnants of salty tear stains on her cheeks. Someone had cleaned her, dressed her.

Ignoring the odd decoration, disinterested in ornamentation, she untangled her legs from the pleated, translucent gown knotted at her throat and stood.

The ground was warm as if it had been heated by sunlight, her feet, painted gold, a similar shade.

Stiff, stepping towards the nearest gaping view, all that was to be seen was ocean. Vast, endless turquoise lapped at the side of the rounded cliff her gilded cage had been carved into. There was nothing to swim to, no sign of hovercraft or spaceship, only birds circling, and water creatures playing near the milder break.

The single interior door was the only other available route.

There was no electric panel or vid display to help her navigate its unbolting, only an archaic lever. Under her fingertips, ancient mechanics etched into the wood gave when she pressed down.

The door was not locked.

Sliding it open, she found a circular anteroom as bizarre as anyone might imagine. The visual curio was segmented into quadrants depicting the seasons of old Earth. She was standing in Summer, gazing up to find a fresco painted on the ceiling above her—cartwheeling gods from a culture she did not know smiled down in their glory.

In the center of the room, a fountain spouted crystal clear water, but that was not what drew her attention. It was the walls of gilded mirrors and the stranger reflected in them. Gone were the dyed lavender eyes, and in their place the icy vibrancy of a glacier. Gone was the sheared skull. Instead, waves hung past her waist. All the pigments Quinn had used to alter her hair into any shade but her own had been leached away, displaying the ethereal brilliance of pale silvery blonde—a shade she had not seen herself since she was a child.

She touched the cool glass.

Nothing looked familiar. The woman reflected was a ghost, an alien.

"Is it so strange?"

Red-rimmed eyes cut to the reflection across the room. She offered the smallest of nods, her attention returning to her image.

No sound accompanied his approach, only the growing size of the uniformed male dwarfing her figure in the mirror. Sovereign was so much taller, boasting a body that spoke of great strength, while her pale reflection was lissome, a wraith with a face of misery and disorientation.

Where she was fragmented, he radiated wholeness, authority.

Eyes far deeper than the ocean she'd glimpsed out of the window tracked over her appearance, full of that same unwelcome tenderness she had first seen years ago.

He asked, "Is there any lingering pain?"

Voice low and lifeless, she pointed to her heart. "Here."

Tears slipped over her cheeks, collecting at her chin to fall on the floor. "Where have you brought me?"

"Somewhere secure. A palace where you can find rest." Voice gentle, mind calm, Sovereign added, "There was a great deal of damage to your brain from the psionic burst that even your rapid healing could not fully counter. You've been asleep for forty-seven years. During that time there were operations, gene therapy, augmentation."

Large eyes burned, filling with hate. "Trying to rectify the mistake you made while I was in gestation?"

The man reached out and brushed the back of his fingers down her long tangle of silvery hair.

"Yes."

She could sense his intention. He was goading her on purpose, testing to see how close she might be to losing control. But he was not completely false. She could feel the oddest heat against the left side of her skull. They *had* put something inside her. "It's a pity you could not cut out my memory too."

His emotions projected agreement, though Sovereign did not voice his opinion aloud. "The psionic centers of your brain have been fitted with suppression technology that will disperse overload. With practice, tailored psionic ability will be available to you now."

Looking to the warming line atop her skull, she imagined where a long circular scar would have developed had she been human. Unimpressed, numb, she muttered, "I have never so long... It doesn't feel as if so much time has passed."

Sovereign's fingertips tucked a lock of hair behind her ear, his voice thick with sentiment. "I felt every hour."

She would feel every last painful crawling hour without her companion, and that thought was awful. "There is no sort of life worth living without Que."

The heat of his hand settled on her shoulder, a thumb dipping under her hair to gently stroke her nape. "I would never have killed him. I want you to know that. I would never have willingly given you such pain."

The sincerity of the emperor's soft spoken words scorched her. Visibly cringing, wanting to dump the blame at his feet, she accused him of his greater slight. "You should have let me die."

"Quinn did die. Sigil was reborn—the past burned away."

Forlorn, her voice broke. "I don't want to be Sigil..."

Poisoned words were softly offered. "Do you want to be Quinn without Que?"

It felt as if he'd ripped straight through her ribcage. As if Sovereign brutally squeezed her heart as she'd once pulverized Drinta's. "No." Her face contorted into one of pain. "Quinn could never survive without him."

The rich compulsion in his voice made the answer seem so simple. "Then they both must be mourned and set aside. As it is now, you have so many reasons to live." He applied more pressure, parting her vertebrae gently. Sovereign purposefully fostered her comfort until the female's shoulders relaxed. "All these years, your Brothers have kept vigil. All the love you seek awaits your recognition."

"Had I the energy, I would kill you, Sovereign. I would move room by room through wherever you've stashed me, slaughtering every remnant of Project Cataclysm that crossed my path."

A gracious smile was offered, Sovereign seemingly pleased with her threats. "I have a gift for you, something that will require a gentle hand." He turned towards the segment of Winter. "Come forward, child."

Another mirror displayed the shy flash of yellow scales. The boy, her Tessan boy she'd left in the cryotube on Pax, ambled nervously forward.

From his anxious expression, he'd heard her threats and openly he feared her.

Guilt found a way to worm through her grief. Memories of Pax, of her outburst... of all the life she'd squelched bubbled up.

"The boy has been in full cryo, waiting for you to wake and decide his fate." Sovereign gestured for the child to come closer.

Mincing steps of a born slave obeyed the summons, his obvious terror softening the horrified expression on Sigil's face.

She took the smallest step toward the emperor, using his body as if to shield the child from herself. "Do you know me, boy?"

There was no answer. The little one was frightened, more than unsure, his tail making little flicks behind him against the cool Winter floor.

Her imaginings for him had been simple: a warm home in an outlying Tessan colony where fresh life was needed. Not this.

The young male looked up at her and she sensed what he truly desired. He wanted his mother.

And Sigil had killed her… had been the cause of the deaths of tens of thousands on Pax.

"The Imperial Consort asked you a question, Jerla." That was not a tone Sigil had ever heard Sovereign employ. It was the tenor one used to guide children. It was a voice of reason and comfort.

The Tessan child shook his head no.

Grief of another sort welled until Sigil felt pinpricks behind her eyes. "I know you, Jerla, son of the slave Ragi." Sovereign dared to slip an arm around her as she spoke, as if to restrain her, to hold her, all the while his terrible mind echoing feelings of reassurance while she spoke. "I have known you since you were birthed. I was the one who hid billop eggs near your sleeping mat when you were good."

His vertical eyelids blinked, the child excited by the mention of his favorite treat. "I liked that game."

"So did I."

Another touch from the emperor, gentle fingers threaded into her hair. Sigil wanted to retaliate, to shove him off, but was too busy staring at the child.

She forced the smallest of smiles. "Have you been happy since you woke?"

Those shining black eyes blinked at her, the male too young to understand. "I get to eat whenever I am hungry."

A slave's version of bliss.

"When I was only a little older than you, I was trapped on a world alone for many years, very hungry."

Innocent, Jerla asked, "Why?"

Sigil's smile faded, sadness returning. "My ship was shot down by bad men. Do you know the difference between bad men and good men?"

How could he? All he had ever known was Pax, drudgery, and neglect. Even so, Jerla nodded in agreement.

"I killed all of those men, lived in the ruins of their outpost until a stranger found me… a good man. The first I had ever met."

The boy's tale swished in interest at her tale. "How did you know he was good?"

Sigil swallowed. "He was the opposite of me in every way."

"You were not good?"

"No," Sigil shook her head, expression grim. "I was not good."

Fear crept into those pitch eyes again.

Sovereign held her tighter, a warning that she must desist from her path. "And she seeks to atone, Jerla. That is why she saved you from the destruction of Pax."

That is not why she had saved him, but Sigil was not going to damage the friendless thing further.

Gentleness leached from Sovereign's voice, replaced with deep-voiced authority. "Thank her quickly, Jerla. The Imperial Consort requires rest."

Shifting foot to foot, his bare little toes clicking on the stone floor, Jerla looked unsure. "Thanks."

Already pulling Sigil towards the Spring segment of the circular anteroom, Sovereign instructed, "Off with you now. You can play with her when she is feeling better."

Where the Tessan child went, Sigil did not see. She was simply glad he was gone. It had been too much, she was too empty, and so she let Sovereign lead her through an open arch into another room.

The sleeping chamber had been Summer, but the dining hall—walls laden with edible growing things and latticed windows overlooking that same endless sea—was clearly Spring.

Food already waited on the table, the dishes beyond Sigil's experience to recognize. Placed in a chair, Sovereign was wise enough to only hand her water. "What made you chose that child over all the young ones on Pax?"

She didn't answer. Cup at her lips, she swallowed, eyes locked on a round deep purple fruit growing nearby.

"That is a mangosteen. According to old Earth legend, inside the shell is something soft that tastes of extinct berries. It is an extreme rarity in these times."

Resigned, Sigil sighed. "With all your planets, you could find a climate to host forests of any fancy fruit you wanted."

"Ecosystems, like politics, are tricky things. New plant life can unbalance whole worlds in less than one human generation."

"So can Irdesian forced Conversion."

Sovereign had the gall to laugh. "True." Reaching past her, he plucked a mangosteen as if the table before him was not ripe with food.

There was an art to opening the fruit, to revealing the soft pale flesh hidden behind its thick shell. He showed her this before offering a piece. "Here."

The odd segment smelt of nula milk, a thing she'd once craved. "No."

Shrugging, Sovereign took the flesh and ate it, leaning back in his chair to watch his female pretend she was not crying. "You have to eat to stay strong. You need to eat so you might guide Jerla's path."

"He doesn't belong amongst humans."

"Why? They have shown him more care than any creature on Pax did."

Insulted, Sigil's head swung towards the irritation snacking at her side. "I cared for him on Pax."

Meeting her eyes, Sovereign conceded. "You did. And he will see to you here in return."

She knew what he was about. "Jerla is only a child. It is wrong for you to use him in such a way."

The man shook his head, his dark hair shifting like the waves outside. "You killed his mother. You exterminated every last lifeform on Pax. He's all that's left."

She thinned her lips to stop them from trembling. "I didn't mean to."

There was a trace of pity reflected in the hardness of his expression. "I know."

He held up what remained of the fruit in offering.

Sigil took a slimy sliver, chewed and swallowed, tasting nothing. "I know what you're doing."

Any creature who has survived torture understood the stage where their assailant built rapport. Sovereign nodded. "I know."

"Are you going to rape me now?"

Those eyes, those deep, strange eyes looked unbelievably sad. "You were not cured of your compulsion. Such a thing was ingrained into your very thinking and chemical response to various stimuli. Do you want to be left feral in a cage with no future? Or do you want freedom and life?"

She let him see how weak she'd become. "I want to go home..."

"Que is dead. You have no home."

Read Sovereign Now!

Addison Cain

USA TODAY bestselling author and Amazon Top 25 bestselling author, Addison Cain is best known for her dark romances, smoldering Omegaverse, and twisted alien worlds. Her antiheroes are not always redeemable, her lead females stand fierce, and nothing is ever as it seems.

Deep and sometimes heart wrenching, her books are not for the faint of heart. But they are just right for those who enjoy unapologetic bad boys, aggressive alphas, and a hint of violence in a kiss.

Visit her website: addisoncain.com

Sign up for my newsletter:

http://bit.ly/AddisonCainNewsletter

Amazon: amzn.to/2ryj4LH
Goodreads: www.goodreads.com/AddisonCain
Bookbub Deals: www.bookbub.com/authors/addison-cain
Facebook Author Page:
www.facebook.com/AddisonlCain/
Addison Cain's Dark Longings Lounge Fan Group:
www.facebook.com/groups/DarkLongingsLounge/

Don't miss these exciting titles by Addison Cain!

Omegaverse:
The Golden Line

The Alpha's Claim Series:
Born to be Bound
Born To Be Broken
Reborn
Stolen
Corrupted (coming soon)

Wren's Song Series:
Branded Captive
Silent Captive
Broken Captive
Ravaged Captive

The Irdesi Empire Series:
Sigil
Sovereign
Que (coming soon)

Cradle of Darkness
Catacombs
Cathedral
The Relic

A Trick of the Light Duet:

A Taste of Shine
A Shot in the Dark

Historical Romance:
Dark Side of the Sun

Horror:
The White Queen
Immaculate

CPSIA information can be obtained
at www.ICGtesting.com
Printed in the USA
FSHW010501130120
66033FS

9 781950 711178